William Shakespeare's
Anthony and Cleopatra
In Plain and Simple English

A SwipeSpeare™ Book
www.SwipeSpeare.com

Table of Contents:

About This Series

The "SwipeSpeare™" series started as a way of telling Shakespeare for the modern reader—being careful to preserve the themes and integrity of the original. Visit our website SwipeSpeare.com to see other books in the series, as well as the interactive, and swipe-able, app!

The series is expanding every month. Visit BookCaps.com to see non-Shakespeare books in this series, and while you are there join the Facebook page, so you are first to know when a new book comes out.

Characters

M.ANTONY, Triumvir
OCTAVIUS CAESAR, Triumvir
M. AEMIL. LEPIDUS, Triumvir
SEXTUS POMPEIUS Triumvir
DOMITIUS ENOBARBUS, friend to Antony
VENTIDIUS, friend to Antony
EROS, friend to Antony
SCARUS, friend to Antony
DERCETAS, friend to Antony
DEMETRIUS, friend to Antony
PHILO, friend to Antony
MAECENAS, friend to Caesar
AGRIPPA, friend to Caesar
DOLABELLA, friend to Caesar
PROCULEIUS, friend to Caesar
THYREUS, friend to Caesar
GALLUS, friend to Caesar
MENAS, friend to Pompey
MENECRATES, friend to Pompey
VARRIUS, friend to Pompey
TAURUS, Lieutenant-General to Caesar
CANIDIUS, Lieutenant-General to Antony
SILIUS, an Officer in Ventidius's army
EUPHRONIUS, an Ambassador from Antony to Caesar
ALEXAS, attendant on Cleopatra
MARDIAN, attendant on Cleopatra
SELEUCUS, attendant on Cleopatra
DIOMEDES, attendant on Cleopatra
A SOOTHSAYER
A CLOWN
CLEOPATRA, Queen of Egypt
OCTAVIA, sister to Caesar and wife to Antony
CHARMIAN, Attendant on Cleopatra
IRAS, Attendant on Cleopatra
Officers, Soldiers, Messengers, and other Attendants

Play

ACT I

SCENE I. Alexandria. A room in CLEOPATRA's palace.

Enter DEMETRIUS and PHILO

PHILO
Nay, but this dotage of our general's
O'erflows the measure: those his goodly eyes,
That o'er the files and musters of the war
Have glow'd like plated Mars, now bend, now turn,

The office and devotion of their view
Upon a tawny front: his captain's heart,
Which in the scuffles of great fights hath burst
The buckles on his breast, reneges all temper,

And is become the bellows and the fan
To cool a gipsy's lust.

No, but this silly devotion of our general's
Is way too much: his good eyes
That over the business of war
Glowed like armored Mars [Roman god of war],
now bend, now turn
The job and devotion of what they look at
Are in a dark direction: his captain's heart,
Which in the battles of huge fights have burst
The buckles on his chest, he no longer has any
passion for war,
And has become the way to manipulate
A dark woman's lust.

Flourish. Enter ANTONY, CLEOPATRA, her Ladies, the Train, with Eunuchs fanning her

Look, where they come:
Take but good note, and you shall see in him.
The triple pillar of the world transform'd
Into a strumpet's fool: behold and see.

Look, see them come:
Just pay attention, and you will see it in him.
The ruler and strength of the world transformed
Into a slut's fool: look and see.

CLEOPATRA
If it be love indeed, tell me how much.

If it really is love, tell me how much.

MARK ANTONY
There's beggary in the love that can be reckon'd.

Any love that could easily be summarized is not
much at all.

CLEOPATRA
I'll set a bourn how far to be beloved.

I'll send a ship as far as your love.

MARK ANTONY
Then must thou needs find out new heaven, new earth.

Then you would have to find a new heaven, a new
earth.

Enter an Attendant

Attendant
News, my good lord, from Rome.
MARK ANTONY
Grates me: the sum.

There is news, sir, from Rome.

I'm busy: be brief.

CLEOPATRA
Nay, hear them, Antony:
Fulvia perchance is angry; or, who knows
If the scarce-bearded Caesar have not sent
His powerful mandate to you, 'Do this, or this;
Take in that kingdom, and enfranchise that;
Perform 't, or else we damn thee.'

MARK ANTONY
How, my love!

CLEOPATRA
Perchance! nay, and most like:
You must not stay here longer, your dismission
Is come from Caesar; therefore hear it, Antony.
Where's Fulvia's process? Caesar's I would say? both?

Call in the messengers. As I am Egypt's queen,

Thou blushest, Antony; and that blood of thine
Is Caesar's homager: else so thy cheek pays shame
When shrill-tongued Fulvia scolds. The messengers!

MARK ANTONY
Let Rome in Tiber melt, and the wide arch
Of the ranged empire fall! Here is my space.

Kingdoms are clay: our dungy earth alike
Feeds beast as man: the nobleness of life

Is to do thus; when such a mutual pair
[Embracing]
And such a twain can do't, in which I bind,

On pain of punishment, the world to weet
We stand up peerless.

CLEOPATRA
Excellent falsehood!
Why did he marry Fulvia, and not love her?
I'll seem the fool I am not; Antony
Will be himself.
MARK ANTONY
But stirr'd by Cleopatra.
Now, for the love of Love and her soft hours,
Let's not confound the time with conference harsh:
There's not a minute of our lives should stretch
Without some pleasure now. What sport tonight?

No, listen to them, Antony:
It is possible Fulvia is angry; or, who knows
If the thinly-bearded Caesar has not sent
His powerful orders to you, "Do this, or this;
Conquer that kingdom, and make that happen;
Perform it, or else we condemn you."

How, my love?

Possibly! And even more likely,
You must not stay here longer, your order to leave
Has come from Caesar; so listen to it, Antony.
Where is Fulvia's procession? Or I should say
Caesar's? Both?
Call in the messengers. As truly as I am Egypt's
queen,
You blush, Antony; and that blood of yours
Honors Caesar: or else your cheek shows shame
When sharp-tongued Fulvia scolds. The
messengers!

May Rome melt in the summer, and the wide arch
Of the boundaries of the empire fall! Here is my
place.
Kingdoms are just dirt: our common soil
Feeds animals the way it does humans: the noble
thing in life
Is to act like this; when such a well-matched pair

And two such people can do it, in which I tie
together,
Even at the risk of punishment, to the world
We are without compare.

What a sweet lie!
Why did he marry Fulvia, only to betray her?
I'll seem more foolish than I am; Antony
Will be himself.

But inspired by Cleopatra.
Now, for the love of Love and her pleasant times,
Let's not spoil things with serious business:
There isn't a minute of our lives that should go by
Without some pleasure now. What fun shall we
have tonight?

CLEOPATRA

Hear the ambassadors.

Listen to the ambassadors.

MARK ANTONY

Fie, wrangling queen!
Whom every thing becomes, to chide, to laugh,
To weep; whose every passion fully strives
To make itself, in thee, fair and admired!
No messenger, but thine; and all alone
To-night we'll wander through the streets and note
The qualities of people. Come, my queen;
Last night you did desire it: speak not to us.

Oh come on, bossy queen!
Who has become everything, to scold, to laugh,
To cry; whose every emotion tries its best
To make itself, in you, beautiful and admired!
No messenger but you; and all alone
Tonight we'll wander through the streets
And observe the people. Come, my queen;
Last night you wanted it: do not talk to us.

Exeunt MARK ANTONY and CLEOPATRA with their train

DEMETRIUS

Is Caesar with Antonius prized so slight?

Does Antony value Caesar so little?

PHILO

Sir, sometimes, when he is not Antony,
He comes too short of that great property
Which still should go with Antony.

Sir, sometimes, when he is not being himself,
He comes up short of the mark
That should be expected of him.

DEMETRIUS

I am full sorry
That he approves the common liar, who
Thus speaks of him at Rome: but I will hope

Of better deeds to-morrow. Rest you happy!

I am very sorry
That he confirms the common rumors
That say such things of him in Rome: but I will
hope
For better things tomorrow. Have a good evening!

Exeunt

SCENE II. The same. Another room.

Enter CHARMIAN, IRAS, ALEXAS, and a Soothsayer

CHARMIAN
Lord Alexas, sweet Alexas, most any thing Alexas,

almost most absolute Alexas, where's the soothsayer

that you praised so to the queen? O, that I knew

this husband, which, you say, must charge his horns
with garlands!

Lord Alexas, wonderful Alexas, best of everything Alexas,
every amazing thing Alexas, where's the fortuneteller
that you praised so much to the queen? Oh, if only I knew
this husband, who, you say, must decorate his horns with garlands!

ALEXAS
Soothsayer!

Fortuneteller!

Soothsayer
Your will?

What do you wish?

CHARMIAN
Is this the man? Is't you, sir, that know things?

Is this the man? Is it you, sir, who knows things?

Soothsayer
In nature's infinite book of secrecy
A little I can read.

Of nature's unlimited secrets
I know a few.

ALEXAS
Show him your hand.

Show him your hand.

Enter DOMITIUS ENOBARBUS

DOMITIUS ENOBARBUS
Bring in the banquet quickly; wine enough
Cleopatra's health to drink.

Bring in the feast quickly: with enough wine
to toast Cleopatra.

CHARMIAN
Good sir, give me good fortune.
Soothsayer
I make not, but foresee.

Good sir, tell me a good fortune.

I do not make fortunes, just see them.

CHARMIAN
Pray, then, foresee me one.

Please, then, see mine.

Soothsayer
You shall be yet far fairer than you are.

You shall someday be more attractive than you are.

CHARMIAN
He means in flesh.

He means in appearance.

IRAS
No, you shall paint when you are old.

No, you shall wear makeup when you are old.

CHARMIAN
Wrinkles forbid!

May I never get wrinkles!

ALEXAS
Vex not his prescience; be attentive.

Don't annoy his wisdom; pay attention.

CHARMIAN
Hush!

Quiet!

Soothsayer
You shall be more beloving than beloved.

You will love more than you are loved.

CHARMIAN
I had rather heat my liver with drinking.

I would rather poison my liver with drinking.

ALEXAS
Nay, hear him.

No, listen to him.

CHARMIAN
Good now, some excellent fortune! Let me be married

to three kings in a forenoon, and widow them all:

let me have a child at fifty, to whom Herod of Jewry

may do homage: find me to marry me with Octavius
Caesar, and companion me with my mistress.

Good, now tell me an excellent fortune! Let me be married
to three kings in a morning, and be the widow of them all.
let me have a child when I am fifty, to whom Herod of the Jews
may honor: find out that I will marry Octavius Caesar, and make me as good as my lady.

Soothsayer
You shall outlive the lady whom you serve.

You will live longer than the lady you serve.

CHARMIAN
O excellent! I love long life better than figs.

Oh, excellent! I love living long better than I love figs.

Soothsayer
You have seen and proved a fairer former fortune
Than that which is to approach.

You have seen and had a more attractive former fortune Than the one that is coming.

CHARMIAN
Then belike my children shall have no names:
prithee, how many boys and wenches must I have?

Then it seems my children shall have no names: please, how many boys and girls will I have?

Soothsayer
If every of your wishes had a womb.
And fertile every wish, a million.

CHARMIAN
Out, fool! I forgive thee for a witch.

ALEXAS
You think none but your sheets are privy to your wishes.

CHARMIAN
Nay, come, tell Iras hers.

ALEXAS
We'll know all our fortunes.

DOMITIUS ENOBARBUS
Mine, and most of our fortunes, to-night, shall be--drunk to bed.

IRAS
There's a palm presages chastity, if nothing else.

CHARMIAN
E'en as the o'erflowing Nilus presageth famine.

IRAS
Go, you wild bedfellow, you cannot soothsay.

CHARMIAN
Nay, if an oily palm be not a fruitful prognostication, I cannot scratch mine ear. Prithee, tell her but a worky-day fortune.

Soothsayer
Your fortunes are alike.

IRAS
But how, but how? give me particulars.

Soothsayer
I have said.

IRAS
Am I not an inch of fortune better than she?

CHARMIAN
Well, if you were but an inch of fortune better than I, where would you choose it?

If every one of your wishes had a womb,
And every wish was fertile, a million.

Out, you fool! I think you're a witch.

You think no one but your bedsheets know your wishes.

No, come, tell Iras hers.

We'll find out all our fortunes.

Mine, and most of our fortunes tonight, shall be passing out drunk.

There's a palm that promises chastity, if nothing else.

The same way the overflowing Nile promises famine.

Go away, you wild roommate, you cannot tell fortunes.

No, if an oily palm is not a fruitful sign of the future, I cannot scratch my ear. Please, just tell her an ordinary everyday fortune.

Your fortunes are all the same.

But how, but how? Give me specifics.

I have.

Am I not even a little bit luckier than her?

Well, if you were only an inch of luck better than me, where would you want it?

IRAS

Not in my husband's nose.

Not as part of my husband's nose.

CHARMIAN

Our worser thoughts heavens mend! Alexas,--come,

his fortune, his fortune! O, let him marry a woman

that cannot go, sweet Isis, I beseech thee! and let
her die too, and give him a worse! and let worst

follow worse, till the worst of all follow him
laughing to his grave, fifty-fold a cuckold! Good

Isis, hear me this prayer, though thou deny me a

matter of more weight; good Isis, I beseech thee!

*May heaven forgive our worse thoughts! Alxas, --
come,
tell his fortune, his fortune! Oh, let him marry a
woman
that cannot go, sweet Isis, I beg you! and let
her die too, and give him worse one! and let even
worse
come after worse, until the worst of all follows him
laughing to his grave, a victim of adultery fifty
times! Good
Isis, hear this prayer from me, even if you don't
give me
something more important; good Isis, I beg you!*

IRAS

Amen. Dear goddess, hear that prayer of the people!

for, as it is a heartbreaking to see a handsome man

loose-wived, so it is a deadly sorrow to behold a
foul knave uncuckolded: therefore, dear Isis, keep
decorum, and fortune him accordingly!

*Amen. Beloved goddess, listen to that prayer of the
people!
for, just as it is a heartbreaking sight to see a
handsome man
with an unfaithful wife, it is also terribly sad to see
a terrible man not betrayed by his wife: therefore,
dear Isis, keep your manners, and give him the
luck he deserves!*

CHARMIAN

Amen.

I agree.

ALEXAS

Lo, now, if it lay in their hands to make me a
cuckold, they would make themselves whores, but

they'ld do't!

*See, now, if it were possible for them to make me a
victim of adultery, they would make themselves
prostitutes; they
would certainly do it!*

DOMITIUS ENOBARBUS

Hush! here comes Antony.

Quiet! Here comes Antony.

CHARMIAN

Not he; the queen.

Not him; the queen.

Enter CLEOPATRA

CLEOPATRA

Saw you my lord?

Did you see my lord?

DOMITIUS ENOBARBUS

No, lady.

No, madam.

CLEOPATRA
Was he not here?

Wasn't he here?

CHARMIAN
No, madam.

No, lady.

CLEOPATRA
He was disposed to mirth; but on the sudden
A Roman thought hath struck him. Enobarbus!

He was in a mood for fun; but all of a sudden
A serious thought struck him. Enobarbus!

DOMITIUS ENOBARBUS
Madam?

Lady?

CLEOPATRA
Seek him, and bring him hither.
Where's Alexas?

Look for him, and bring him here.
Where is Alexas?

ALEXAS
Here, at your service. My lord approaches.

Here, at your service. My husband is coming.

CLEOPATRA
We will not look upon him: go with us.

We will not stay with him: go with us.

Exeunt
Enter MARK ANTONY with a Messenger and Attendants

Messenger
Fulvia thy wife first came into the field.

Your wife Fulvia began the battle.

MARK ANTONY
Against my brother Lucius?

Against Lucius, my brother?

Messenger
Ay:
But soon that war had end, and the time's state

Made friends of them, joining their force 'gainst
against Caesar;
Whose better issue in the war, from Italy,
Upon the first encounter, drave them.

Yes:
But soon the war ended, and the changing
circumstances
Made them into friends, joining their forces
Caesar;
Whose best troops in the war, from Italy,
Beat them the first time they met.

MARK ANTONY
Well, what worst?

Well, what could be worse?

Messenger
The nature of bad news infects the teller.

The nature of bad news upsets the messenger.

MARK ANTONY
When it concerns the fool or coward. On:
Things that are past are done with me. 'Tis thus:

When it is about a fool or a coward. Continue:
I don't dwell on the past. It's like this:

Who tells me true, though in his tale lie death,

I hear him as he flatter'd.

Whoever tells me the truth, even if they bring bad news,
I listen as though he were flattering me.

Messenger
Labienus--
This is stiff news--hath, with his Parthian force,

Labienus --
This is difficult news -- has, with his Parthian forces,

Extended Asia from Euphrates;
His conquering banner shook from Syria
To Lydia and to Ionia; Whilst--

Expanded Asia from the Euphrates river;
His conquering flag flies from Syria
To Lydia and to Ionia; While --

MARK ANTONY
Antony, thou wouldst say,--

Antony, you would say, --

Messenger
O, my lord!

Oh, sir!

MARK ANTONY
Speak to me home, mince not the general tongue:
Name Cleopatra as she is call'd in Rome;
Rail thou in Fulvia's phrase; and taunt my faults
With such full licence as both truth and malice
Have power to utter. O, then we bring forth weeds,

Talk to me frankly, do not mince words:
Refer to Cleopatra as they call her in Rome;
Go on in praise of Fulvia; and mock my faults
With the full ability that both truth and hate
Have power to speak. Oh, then we will take offense,

When our quick minds lie still; and our ills told us

When our clever minds lie still; and our flaws are told to us

Is as our earing. Fare thee well awhile.

In our hearing. Goodbye for a while.

Messenger
At your noble pleasure.

As you wish.

Exit

MARK ANTONY
From Sicyon, ho, the news! Speak there!

The news from Sicyon, hey! Speak there!

First Attendant
The man from Sicyon,--is there such an one?

The man from Sicyon, -- is there one?

Second Attendant
He stays upon your will.

He stays because you asked him to.

MARK ANTONY
Let him appear.
These strong Egyptian fetters I must break,
Or lose myself in dotage.

Tell him to come here.
I must break these strong Egyptians chains,
Or lose myself in foolishness.

Enter another Messenger

What are you?

Second Messenger
Fulvia thy wife is dead.

MARK ANTONY
Where died she?

Second Messenger
In Sicyon:
Her length of sickness, with what else more serious

Importeth thee to know, this bears.

Gives a letter

MARK ANTONY
Forbear me.

Exit Second Messenger

There's a great spirit gone! Thus did I desire it:
What our contempt doth often hurl from us,
We wish it ours again; the present pleasure,

By revolution lowering, does become
The opposite of itself: she's good, being gone;

The hand could pluck her back that shoved her on.

I must from this enchanting queen break off:
Ten thousand harms, more than the ills I know,

My idleness doth hatch. How now! Enobarbus!

Re-enter DOMITIUS ENOBARBUS

DOMITIUS ENOBARBUS
What's your pleasure, sir?

MARK ANTONY
I must with haste from hence.

DOMITIUS ENOBARBUS
Why, then, we kill all our women:
we see how mortal an unkindness is to them;
if they suffer our departure, death's the word.

MARK ANTONY
I must be gone.

Where are you from?

Your wife Fulvia is dead.

Where did she die?

In Sicyon:
How long she was sick, and other more serious matters
You need to know, are in this letter.

Leave me alone.

Now a great spirit is gone! I wanted it this way:
What our hatred often throws away from us,
We want it for ourselves again; the current pleasure,
Becomes less as it turns, it becomes
The opposite of itself: she is better now that she is gone;
That hand could pull her back that shoved her away.
I must leave this enchanting queen.
Ten thousand problems, more than the bad things I know,
My lazing around causes. What now! Enobarbus!

What is your wish, sir?

I must quickly leave here.

Why, then, we would kill all our women:
we see how terribly they take any unkindness;
if they must deal with us leaving, they will die.

I must leave.

DOMITIUS ENOBARBUS
Under a compelling occasion, let women die; it were

pity to cast them away for nothing; though, between

them and a great cause, they should be esteemed

nothing. Cleopatra, catching but the least noise of

this, dies instantly; I have seen her die twenty
times upon far poorer moment: I do think there is
mettle in death, which commits some loving act upon
her, she hath such a celerity in dying.

MARK ANTONY
She is cunning past man's thought.

Exit ALEXAS

DOMITIUS ENOBARBUS
Alack, sir, no; her passions are made of nothing but

the finest part of pure love: we cannot call her
winds and waters sighs and tears; they are greater

storms and tempests than almanacs can report: this

cannot be cunning in her; if it be, she makes a
shower of rain as well as Jove.

MARK ANTONY
Would I had never seen her.

DOMITIUS ENOBARBUS
O, sir, you had then left unseen a wonderful piece
of work;

which not to have been blest withal would
have discredited your travel.

MARK ANTONY
Fulvia is dead.

DOMITIUS ENOBARBUS
Sir?

MARK ANTONY
Fulvia is dead.

DOMITIUS ENOBARBUS

If there is a good enough reason, let the women die; it would be
a pity to throw them away for nothing; though, between
them and an important cause, they should be considered
nothing. Cleopatra, hearing the smallest portion of
this, will die instantly; I have seen her die twenty times for a much worse reason: I do think there is courage in death, which gives some loving act to her, she has such a dramatic habit of dying.

She is more cunning than any man could think.

Unfortunately, sir, no; her emotions are made of nothing but
the best part of pure love: we cannot call her winds and waters sighs and tears; they are far more huge
storms and typhoons than almanacs can predict: this
cannot be her being cunning; if it is, she makes a shower of rain as well as Jove [God of storms].

I wish I had never seen her.

Oh, sir, but then you would have not seen a wonderful piece of work;

which to not have been blessed with would have been a shame on your travels.

Fulvia died.

Sir?

Fulvia is dead.

Fulvia!

MARK ANTONY
Dead.

DOMITIUS ENOBARBUS
Why, sir, give the gods a thankful sacrifice. When
it pleaseth their deities to take the wife of a man
from him, it shows to man the tailors of the earth;

comforting therein, that when old robes are worn

out, there are members to make new. If there were
no more women but Fulvia, then had you indeed a cut,

and the case to be lamented: this grief is crowned
with consolation; your old smock brings forth a new

petticoat: and indeed the tears live in an onion

that should water this sorrow.

MARK ANTONY
The business she hath broached in the state
Cannot endure my absence.

DOMITIUS ENOBARBUS
And the business you have broached here cannot be
without you; especially that of Cleopatra's, which
wholly depends on your abode.

MARK ANTONY
No more light answers. Let our officers
Have notice what we purpose. I shall break
The cause of our expedience to the queen,
And get her leave to part. For not alone
The death of Fulvia, with more urgent touches,
Do strongly speak to us; but the letters too
Of many our contriving friends in Rome
Petition us at home: Sextus Pompeius
Hath given the dare to Caesar, and commands
The empire of the sea: our slippery people,
Whose love is never link'd to the deserver
Till his deserts are past, begin to throw

Pompey the Great and all his dignities
Upon his son; who, high in name and power,
Higher than both in blood and life, stands up
For the main soldier: whose quality, going on,

Fulvia?

Dead.

*Well, sir, thank the gods with a sacrifice. When
it pleases the gods to take the wife of a man
from him, it shows to mankind the tailors of the
earth;
comforting them with this, that when old robes are
worn
out, there are new ones made. If there were
no more women except Fulvia, then you would
have an injury indeed,
and we would mourn: this grief instead is topped
with comfort; your old clothes can now be
replaced with new
ones: and indeed there are enough tears in an
onion
to provide water for this sadness.*

*The business she has begun in politics
Cannot stand my being away.*

*And the business you have begun here cannot be
without you; especially Cleopatra's, which
completely depends on where you live.*

*No more silliness. Let our officers
Know what we intend to do. I will break
The news of our required actions to the queen,
And get her permission to leave. For it is not only
The death of Fulvia, with more urgent reasons,
Speak to us strongly; but also the many letters
That our friends in Rome
Demand we come home: Sextus Pompeius
Has challenged Caesar, and orders
The empire of the sea: our unfaithful people,
Whose love is never for the person who deserves it
Until he no longer deserves it, have begun to
throw
Pompey the Great and all this authority
Upon his won; who, high up in name and power,
Higher than both in ancestry and life, stands up
For the common soldier: whose quality, going on,*

The sides o' the world may danger: much is breeding,

Which, like the courser's hair, hath yet but life,
And not a serpent's poison. Say, our pleasure,
To such whose place is under us, requires
Our quick remove from hence.

DOMITIUS ENOBARBUS
I shall do't.

Exeunt

The borders of the world may put in danger: there is much in heritage,
Which, like the horse's hair, has still only life,
And not a snake's poison. Say, what we want,
To those whose position is under us, requires
Us to leave here quickly.

I will do it.

SCENE III. The same. Another room.

Enter CLEOPATRA, CHARMIAN, IRAS, and ALEXAS

CLEOPATRA
Where is he?

Where is he?

CHARMIAN
I did not see him since.

I have not seen him recently.

CLEOPATRA
See where he is, who's with him, what he does:
I did not send you: if you find him sad,
Say I am dancing; if in mirth, report
That I am sudden sick: quick, and return.

See where he is, who is with him, what he is doing:
Pretend I didn't send you: if you find him sad,
Say I am dancing; if having fun, tell him
That I am suddenly sick: be quick, and return.

Exit ALEXAS

CHARMIAN
Madam, methinks, if you did love him dearly,
You do not hold the method to enforce
The like from him.

Madam, I think if you did love him dearly,
You would not try all these things to force
His emotions and liking.

CLEOPATRA
What should I do, I do not?

What should I do if I didn't?

CHARMIAN
In each thing give him way, cross him nothing.

Give him everything he wants; don't go against
him in anything.

CLEOPATRA
Thou teachest like a fool; the way to lose him.

You teach like a fool; that is the way to lose him.

CHARMIAN
Tempt him not so too far; I wish, forbear:

In time we hate that which we often fear.
But here comes Antony.

Do not manipulate him too much; please, hold
back:
We eventually come to hate what we often fear.
But here Antony comes.

Enter MARK ANTONY

CLEOPATRA
I am sick and sullen.

I am sick and in a bad mood.

MARK ANTONY
I am sorry to give breathing to my purpose,--

I am sorry to speak aloud what I need to do, --

CLEOPATRA
Help me away, dear Charmian; I shall fall:
It cannot be thus long, the sides of nature
Will not sustain it.

MARK ANTONY
Now, my dearest queen,--

CLEOPATRA
Pray you, stand further from me.

MARK ANTONY
What's the matter?

CLEOPATRA
I know, by that same eye, there's some good news.
What says the married woman? You may go:
Would she had never given you leave to come!

Let her not say 'tis I that keep you here:
I have no power upon you; hers you are.

MARK ANTONY
The gods best know,--

CLEOPATRA
O, never was there queen
So mightily betray'd! yet at the first
I saw the treasons planted.

MARK ANTONY
Cleopatra,--

CLEOPATRA
Why should I think you can be mine and true,
Though you in swearing shake the throned gods,
Who have been false to Fulvia? Riotous madness,
To be entangled with those mouth-made vows,
Which break themselves in swearing!

MARK ANTONY
Most sweet queen,--

CLEOPATRA
Nay, pray you, seek no colour for your going,
But bid farewell, and go: when you sued staying,

Then was the time for words: no going then;

Eternity was in our lips and eyes,

Help me leave, dear Charmian; I will faint:
It can't be long from now, the laws of nature
Will not keep it going

Now, my beloved queen, --

Please, stand further away from me.

What's the matter?

I know by your face that there's some good news.
What does the married woman say? You may go:
I wish she had never given you permission to come!
May she not say that I keep you here:
I have no power over you; you are hers.

The gods know best,--

Oh, there was never a queen
Betrayed so much! Yet from the beginning
I saw the betrayal begun.

Cleopatra,--

Why should I think you can be mine and faithful,
Even if you swear by all the gods,
You who have betrayed Fulvia? Chaotic madness,
To be mixed up with those promises spoken,
Which break themselves as they are being sworn!

Sweetest queen,--

No, please, don't look for permission to leave,
But say goodbye, and go: when you begged to stay,
That was the time for words: you wouldn't go then;
Our lips and eyes saw forever,

Bliss in our brows' bent; none our parts so poor,

But was a race of heaven: they are so still,
Or thou, the greatest soldier of the world,
Art turn'd the greatest liar.

MARK ANTONY
How now, lady!

CLEOPATRA
I would I had thy inches; thou shouldst know

There were a heart in Egypt.

MARK ANTONY
Hear me, queen:
The strong necessity of time commands
Our services awhile; but my full heart

Remains in use with you. Our Italy
Shines o'er with civil swords: Sextus Pompeius
Makes his approaches to the port of Rome:
Equality of two domestic powers
Breed scrupulous faction: the hated, grown to strength,
Are newly grown to love: the condemn'd Pompey,
Rich in his father's honour, creeps apace,
Into the hearts of such as have not thrived
Upon the present state, whose numbers threaten;

And quietness, grown sick of rest, would purge
By any desperate change: my more particular,

And that which most with you should safe my going,

Is Fulvia's death.

CLEOPATRA
Though age from folly could not give me freedom,

It does from childishness: can Fulvia die?

MARK ANTONY
She's dead, my queen:
Look here, and at thy sovereign leisure read
The garboils she awaked; at the last, best:
See when and where she died.

CLEOPATRA
O most false love!
Where be the sacred vials thou shouldst fill

*Perfect happiness in our faces; none of our parts,
however unimportant
Were less than heavenly: they are still that way,
Or you, the greatest soldier in the world,
Have become the biggest liar.*

What, lady!

*I wish I were as tall and strong as you; you would
know
There is a heart in Egypt.*

*Listen to me, queen:
The importance of quick action will take up
Our time and energy for a while; but my whole
heart
Stays with you. Our Italy
Is struck with civil war: Sextus Pompeius
Is coming to the port of Rome:
The equality of two domestic powers
Have had new results: the hated, now stronger,
Are now allies: the condemned Pompey,
Rich in his father's honor, is creeping
Into the hearts of those who have not done well
Under the current situation, whose numbers are
threatening;
And tired of the peace, would start violence
For any desperate change: and my most important
reason,
And the most important one for you sending me on
my way,
Is Fulvia dying.*

*Though getting older could not save me from
foolishness,
It does from childishness: is it possible for Fulvia
to die?*

*She is dead, my queen:
Look here, and when you have time read
The troubles she awakened; especially at the end:
See where and when she died.*

*Oh most unfaithful love!
Where are your tears?*

With sorrowful water? Now I see, I see,
In Fulvia's death, how mine received shall be.

MARK ANTONY
Quarrel no more, but be prepared to know
The purposes I bear; which are, or cease,
As you shall give the advice. By the fire
That quickens Nilus' slime, I go from hence
Thy soldier, servant; making peace or war
As thou affect'st.

CLEOPATRA
Cut my lace, Charmian, come;
But let it be: I am quickly ill, and well,
So Antony loves.

MARK ANTONY
My precious queen, forbear;
And give true evidence to his love, which stands

An honourable trial.

CLEOPATRA
So Fulvia told me.
I prithee, turn aside and weep for her,
Then bid adieu to me, and say the tears
Belong to Egypt: good now, play one scene
Of excellent dissembling; and let it look
Life perfect honour.

MARK ANTONY
You'll heat my blood: no more.

CLEOPATRA
You can do better yet; but this is meetly.

MARK ANTONY
Now, by my sword,--

CLEOPATRA
And target. Still he mends;
But this is not the best. Look, prithee, Charmian,
How this Herculean Roman does become
The carriage of his chafe.

MARK ANTONY
I'll leave you, lady.

CLEOPATRA
Courteous lord, one word.

Where is your sadness? Now I see, I see,
How you would treat my death, through Fulvia's.

Don't argue any longer, but be prepared to know
The intentions I have; which will continue, or stop,
Depending on the advice you give. By the energy
That moves the Nile, I go from here
Your soldier, servant; making peace or war
As you wish.

Help me with my clothes, Charmian, come
But leave it alone: I am quickly ill, and well,
That is how Antony loves.

My precious queen, please hang on;
And give accurate evidence to his love, when it
stands
An honorable trial.

That is what Fulvia told me.
Please, go, and cry for her,
Then say goodbye to me, and say the tears
Belong to Egypt: be good now, play one scene
Of excellent lying; and let it look
Perfectly lifelike honor.

You'll upset me: stop.

You can do better yet; but this is appropriate.

Now, I swear,--

And target. Still he tries to fix;
But this is not the best. Look, please, Charmian,
How this Roman so much like Hercules becomes
The vehicle of his own troubles.

I'll leave you here, lady.

Polite lord, just one word.

Sir, you and I must part, but that's not it:
Sir, you and I have loved, but there's not it;
That you know well: something it is I would,
O, my oblivion is a very Antony,
And I am all forgotten.

MARK ANTONY
But that your royalty
Holds idleness your subject, I should take you

For idleness itself.

CLEOPATRA
'Tis sweating labour
To bear such idleness so near the heart
As Cleopatra this. But, sir, forgive me;
Since my becomings kill me, when they do not
Eye well to you: your honour calls you hence;

Therefore be deaf to my unpitied folly.

And all the gods go with you! upon your sword

Sit laurel victory! and smooth success
Be strew'd before your feet!

MARK ANTONY
Let us go. Come;
Our separation so abides, and flies,
That thou, residing here, go'st yet with me,
And I, hence fleeting, here remain with thee. Away!

Exeunt

Sir, you and I must separate, but that's not it:
Sir, you and I have loved, but that's not it;
You know that well: it is something I want,
Oh, my doom is all Antony,
And I am completely forgotten.

Except for your royalty
Makes not doing anything your subject, I would take you
For inaction itself.

It is sweating labor
To bring such inaction so near the heart
As this does to Cleopatra. But, sir, forgive me;
Since my good qualities kill me, when they do not
Seem good to you: your honor calls you from here;
Therefore do not listen to my foolishness no one pities.
And may all the gods go with you! May your sword
Have victory! And may smooth success
Be spread under your feet!

Let's go. Come on;
Are separation will be like this,
That you, staying here, still go with me,
And I, running from here, am still here with you. Away!

SCENE IV. Rome. OCTAVIUS CAESAR's house.

Enter OCTAVIUS CAESAR, reading a letter, LEPIDUS, and their Train

OCTAVIUS CAESAR
You may see, Lepidus, and henceforth know,
It is not Caesar's natural vice to hate
Our great competitor: from Alexandria
This is the news: he fishes, drinks, and wastes

The lamps of night in revel; is not more man-like

Than Cleopatra; nor the queen of Ptolemy
More womanly than he; hardly gave audience, or

Vouchsafed to think he had partners: you shall find there
A man who is the abstract of all faults
That all men follow.

LEPIDUS
I must not think there are
Evils enow to darken all his goodness:
His faults in him seem as the spots of heaven,
More fiery by night's blackness; hereditary,

Rather than purchased; what he cannot change,
Than what he chooses.

OCTAVIUS CAESAR
You are too indulgent. Let us grant, it is not
Amiss to tumble on the bed of Ptolemy;
To give a kingdom for a mirth; to sit
And keep the turn of tippling with a slave;
To reel the streets at noon, and stand the buffet

With knaves that smell of sweat: say this becomes him,--
As his composure must be rare indeed
Whom these things cannot blemish,--yet must Antony

No way excuse his soils, when we do bear
So great weight in his lightness. If he fill'd
His vacancy with his voluptuousness,
Full surfeits, and the dryness of his bones,

You may see, Lepidus, and know from now on,
That it is not Caesar's natural sin to hate
Our enemy: from Alexandria
This is the news: he messes around, drinks, and wastes
The oil in lamps in his late-night parties; he is not more a man
Than Cleopatra; and the queen of Ptolemy
Isn't any more like a woman than him; he hardly paid attention, or
Volunteered the information that he had allies: you will find there
A man who is the example of all flaws
That all people have.

I must not believe there are
Enough evil things to spoil all his goodness:
His faults in him are like the stars in the sky,
More bright in the darkness of nighttime; inherited,
Instead of bought; what he cannot change,
Not what he chooses.

You are too generous. Let us allow that it is not
A problem to tumble on the bed of Ptolemy;
To give away a kingdom for some fun; to sit
And chat with a slave;
To wander the streets at noon, and spend your time
With villains who smell of sweat; say this
is a suitable thing for him, --
Since his dignity must be unusually good indeed
If it cannot be reduced by these things, -- yet Antony
Does not excuse himself at all, when we do carry
Such a big weight when his is so light. If he filled
The things he lacks with the things he has,
Full amounts, and the dryness of his bones,

Call on him for't: but to confound such time,
That drums him from his sport, and speaks as loud
As his own state and ours,--'tis to be chid
As we rate boys, who, being mature in knowledge,

Pawn their experience to their present pleasure,
And so rebel to judgment.

Enter a Messenger

LEPIDUS
Here's more news.

Messenger
Thy biddings have been done; and every hour,

Most noble Caesar, shalt thou have report
How 'tis abroad. Pompey is strong at sea;

And it appears he is beloved of those
That only have fear'd Caesar: to the ports

The discontents repair, and men's reports

Give him much wrong'd.

OCTAVIUS CAESAR
I should have known no less.
It hath been taught us from the primal state,
That he which is was wish'd until he were;

And the ebb'd man, ne'er loved till ne'er worth love,

Comes dear'd by being lack'd. This common body,

Like to a vagabond flag upon the stream,
Goes to and back, lackeying the varying tide,
To rot itself with motion.

Messenger
Caesar, I bring thee word,
Menecrates and Menas, famous pirates,
Make the sea serve them, which they ear and wound

With keels of every kind: many hot inroads
They make in Italy; the borders maritime
Lack blood to think on't, and flush youth revolt:

No vessel can peep forth, but 'tis as soon
Taken as seen; for Pompey's name strikes more

Call on him for it: but to use up such time,
That takes him from his fun, and speaks as loud
As his own situation and ours, -- it is to be scolded
The way we consider boys, who, being mature in
knowledge,
Trade their experience for their current pleasure,
And in that way rebel against better judgment.

Here's some more news.

Your commands have been done; and once every
hour,
Noblest Caesar, you shall have a report
Of how things are abroad. Pompey's forces are
strong at sea'
And it appears that he is loved by those
That have only feared [rather than loved] Caesar:
to the ports
The people who are not content go, and the
reports of him
Say he has been much wronged.

I should have known it.
It has been taught to us from the very beginning,
That he who is in power was wanted until he made
it;
And the man in a bad situation, never loved until
he was never worth love
Becomes loved by being gone. The common
people,
Is like a torn flag floating on the stream,
Going to and fro, traveling with the changing tine,
Rotting with its motion.

Caesar, I bring you news,
Menecrates and Menas, well-known pirates,
Are ruling the sea, where they cut people's ears off
and wound
On all sorts of ships: a lot of progress
They make in Italy; those on the coasts
Do not have the courage to deal with it, and
protest:
No ship can go out without immediately being
Spotted, for Pompey's name means more

Than could his war resisted.

Than his war can be reisisted.

OCTAVIUS CAESAR
Antony,
Leave thy lascivious wassails. When thou once
Wast beaten from Modena, where thou slew'st
Hirtius and Pansa, consuls, at thy heel
Did famine follow; whom thou fought'st against,
Though daintily brought up, with patience more
Than savages could suffer: thou didst drink
The stale of horses, and the gilded puddle
Which beasts would cough at: thy palate then did deign

The roughest berry on the rudest hedge;
Yea, like the stag, when snow the pasture sheets,

The barks of trees thou browsed'st; on the Alps
It is reported thou didst eat strange flesh,
Which some did die to look on: and all this--
It wounds thine honour that I speak it now--
Was borne so like a soldier, that thy cheek

So much as lank'd not.

Mark Antony,
Leave your immoral games. When you once
Were chased from Modena, when you killed
Hirtius and Pansa, officials, after you
Famine followed; which you fought against,
Though raised in comfort, with more patience
Than savages could endure: you drank
Horse urine, and dirty puddles
Which animals would refuse: your appetite was
humble enough
To eat tough berries from tougher bushes;
Yes, like the stag deer, when the pastures are
covered in snow,
You ate the bark of trees; on the Alps
Rumor has it you ate strange meat,
Which some died to see: and all this --
It injures your honor that I say it now --
Was tolerated so much like a soldier, that your
face
Never lost strength.

LEPIDUS
'Tis pity of him.

It is a real shame.

OCTAVIUS CAESAR
Let his shames quickly
Drive him to Rome: 'tis time we twain
Did show ourselves i' the field; and to that end
Assemble we immediate council: Pompey
Thrives in our idleness.

May his shames quickly
Push him to Rome: it is time the two of us
Showed ourselves in the field; and to that purpose
We will immediately gather together: Pompey
Becomes stronger as we do nothing.

LEPIDUS
To-morrow, Caesar,
I shall be furnish'd to inform you rightly
Both what by sea and land I can be able
To front this present time.

Tomorrow, Caesar,
I will have the ability to tell you correctly
What by sea and land I will be able
To manage at this time.

OCTAVIUS CAESAR
Till which encounter,
It is my business too. Farewell.

Until that meeting,
It is my work too. Farewell.

LEPIDUS
Farewell, my lord: what you shall know meantime

Of stirs abroad, I shall beseech you, sir,
To let me be partaker.

Farewell, my lord: whatever you find out in the
meantime
About foreign issues, please, sir,
Fill me in as well.

OCTAVIUS CAESAR
Doubt not, sir;
I knew it for my bond.

Exeunt

Do not doubt it, sir;
I knew it as part of my promise.

SCENE V. Alexandria. CLEOPATRA's palace.

Enter CLEOPATRA, CHARMIAN, IRAS, and MARDIAN

CLEOPATRA
Charmian!

Charmian!

CHARMIAN
Madam?

Madam?

CLEOPATRA
Ha, ha!
Give me to drink mandragora.

Ha ha!
Give me a sleeping potion to drink.

CHARMIAN
Why, madam?

Why, madam?

CLEOPATRA
That I might sleep out this great gap of time
My Antony is away.

So I may sleep away the huge length of time
My Mark Antony is away.

CHARMIAN
You think of him too much.

You think about him too much.

CLEOPATRA
O, 'tis treason!

Oh, that is treason!

CHARMIAN
Madam, I trust, not so.

Madam, I'm sure it isn't.

CLEOPATRA
Thou, eunuch Mardian!

Hey you, Mardian the eunuch!

MARDIAN
What's your highness' pleasure?

What does your highness wish?

CLEOPATRA
Not now to hear thee sing; I take no pleasure

In aught an eunuch has: 'tis well for thee,
That, being unseminar'd, thy freer thoughts
May not fly forth of Egypt. Hast thou affections?

Not to hear you sing right now; I have no
enjoyment
In anything a eunuch has: it is good for you,
That, not having an education, your freer thoughts
Will not go away from Egypt. Do you have
romantic feelings?

MARDIAN
Yes, gracious madam.

Yes, kind lady.

CLEOPATRA
Indeed!

MARDIAN
Not in deed, madam; for I can do nothing

But what indeed is honest to be done:
Yet have I fierce affections, and think
What Venus did with Mars.

CLEOPATRA
O Charmian,
Where think'st thou he is now? Stands he, or sits he?

Or does he walk? or is he on his horse?
O happy horse, to bear the weight of Antony!
Do bravely, horse! for wot'st thou whom thou movest?

The demi-Atlas of this earth, the arm
And burgonet of men. He's speaking now,
Or murmuring 'Where's my serpent of old Nile?'

For so he calls me: now I feed myself
With most delicious poison. Think on me,
That am with Phoebus' amorous pinches black,
And wrinkled deep in time? Broad-fronted Caesar,

When thou wast here above the ground, I was
A morsel for a monarch: and great Pompey
Would stand and make his eyes grow in my brow;
There would he anchor his aspect and die
With looking on his life.

Enter ALEXAS, from OCTAVIUS CAESAR

ALEXAS
Sovereign of Egypt, hail!

CLEOPATRA
How much unlike art thou Mark Antony!
Yet, coming from him, that great medicine hath
With his tinct gilded thee.
How goes it with my brave Mark Antony?

ALEXAS
Last thing he did, dear queen,
He kiss'd,--the last of many doubled kisses,--
This orient pearl. His speech sticks in my heart.

CLEOPATRA

You do?

I have not acted on them, madam; for I can do nothing
Except for what can be honestly done:
Yet I have have passionate feelings, and think
About how Venus did to Mars.

Oh, Charmian,
Where do you think he is now? Is he standing or sitting?
Or is he walking? Or is he on his horse?
Oh, lucky horse, to carry the weight of Antony!
Be brave, horse! For do you know whom you are moving?
The holder-up of this earth, the arm
And ruler of men. He's speaking now,
Or murmuring, "Where is my snake of the old Nile?"
Because he calls me that: now I feed myself
With delicious poison. Think about me,
That am bruised with the pinches of love,
And struggling with time? Wide and strong Caesar,
When you were here above the ground, I was
A small mouthful for a ruler: and great Pompey
Would stand and watch me;
There he would fasten himself and die
From looking at his life.

Leader of Egypt, greetings!

You are so different from Mark Antony!
Yet, since you have come from him, you
Are blessed with his essence.
How is my brave Mark Antony doing?

The last thing he did, dear queen,
He kissed, -- the last of many repeated kisses, --
This Asian pearl. His speech sticks in my heart.

Mine ear must pluck it thence.

My ear must pull it from there.

ALEXAS
'Good friend,' quoth he,
'Say, the firm Roman to great Egypt sends
This treasure of an oyster; at whose foot,
To mend the petty present, I will piece
Her opulent throne with kingdoms; all the east,
Say thou, shall call her mistress.' So he nodded,
And soberly did mount an arm-gaunt steed,

Who neigh'd so high, that what I would have spoke

Was beastly dumb'd by him.

'Good friend,' he says,
'The steady Roman to great Egypt sends
This treasure from an oyster; in front of which,
To make up for that small present, I will surround
Her wealthy throne with kingdoms; all the east,
Shall call her their ruler.' So he nodded,
And in a serious manner climbed up on an armored horse,
Who neighed so loud, that what I would have spoken
Was drowned out by him.

CLEOPATRA
What, was he sad or merry?

What, was he sad, or cheerful?

ALEXAS
Like to the time o' the year between the extremes
Of hot and cold, he was nor sad nor merry.

Like the time of year between the extremes
Of hot and cold, he was neither sad or cheerful.

CLEOPATRA
O well-divided disposition! Note him,
Note him good Charmian, 'tis the man; but note him:

He was not sad, for he would shine on those

That make their looks by his; he was not merry,

Which seem'd to tell them his remembrance lay
In Egypt with his joy; but between both:

O heavenly mingle! Be'st thou sad or merry,

The violence of either thee becomes,
So does it no man else. Met'st thou my posts?

Oh, calm and sensible personality! Notice him,
Notice him good Charmian, it is the man; but notice him;
He was not sad, because he wanted to inspire those
That take their example from him; he was not cheerful,
Which would seem to tell them his heart lay
In Egypt with his joy; but kept his mood between both:
Oh wonderful mixture! Whether you are sad or cheerful,
You become either extreme,
No other man does like him. Did you meet my messengers?

ALEXAS
Ay, madam, twenty several messengers:
Why do you send so thick?

Yes, madam, twenty different messengers:
Why do you send so many at once?

CLEOPATRA
Who's born that day
When I forget to send to Antony,
Shall die a beggar. Ink and paper, Charmian.

Welcome, my good Alexas. Did I, Charmian,
Ever love Caesar so?

Whoever is born the day
When I forget to write to Antony,
Shall die a beggar. Bring me ink and paper, Charmian,
Welcome, my dear Alexas. Did I, Charmian,
Ever love that Caesar so much?

CHARMIAN
O that brave Caesar!

Oh, that brave Caesar!

CLEOPATRA
Be choked with such another emphasis!
Say, the brave Antony.

Be choked if you say something like that again!
Say instead, the brave Antony.

CHARMIAN
The valiant Caesar!

The courageous Caesar!

CLEOPATRA
By Isis, I will give thee bloody teeth,
If thou with Caesar paragon again
My man of men.

By Isis, I will give you bloody teeth,
If you compare with Caesar again,
My ultimate man.

CHARMIAN
By your most gracious pardon,
I sing but after you.

Please kindly forgive me,
I am only following you in praises.

CLEOPATRA
My salad days,
When I was green in judgment: cold in blood,

To say as I said then! But, come, away;
Get me ink and paper:
He shall have every day a several greeting,
Or I'll unpeople Egypt.

My younger days,
When I was inexperienced in judgement: cold in blood,
To say what I said then! But, come on, let's go:
Fetch me ink and paper:
I will send him a different greeting each day,
Or I'll make Egypt have no people.

Exeunt

SCENE I. Messina. POMPEY's house.

Enter POMPEY, MENECRATES, and MENAS, in warlike manner

POMPEY
If the great gods be just, they shall assist
The deeds of justest men.

If the great gods are fair, they will help
The actions of fair men.

MENECRATES
Know, worthy Pompey,
That what they do delay, they not deny.

You should know, worthy Pompey,
That the things they delay, they don't deny.

POMPEY
Whiles we are suitors to their throne, decays

The thing we sue for.

While we are contenders to their throne, it slowly
ruins
The thing we are trying to get.

MENECRATES
We, ignorant of ourselves,
Beg often our own harms, which the wise powers

Deny us for our good; so find we profit

By losing of our prayers.

We, unaware of ourselves,
Often ask for things that will harm us, which wise
powers
Keep away from us for our own good; so we find
out we benefit
By not getting our prayers.

POMPEY
I shall do well:
The people love me, and the sea is mine;
My powers are crescent, and my auguring hope

Says it will come to the full. Mark Antony
In Egypt sits at dinner, and will make
No wars without doors: Caesar gets money where

He loses hearts: Lepidus flatters both,
Of both is flatter'd; but he neither loves,
Nor either cares for him.

I will succeed:
The people love me, and my navy rules the sea:
My powers are growing, and my hopeful
prediction
Says they will become full. Mark Antony
Sits at dinner in Egypt, and will make
No wars without opportunities: Caesar gets money
where
He loses loyalty: Lepidus flatters both,
And is flattered by both, but he loves neither,
And neither of them cares for him.

MENAS
Caesar and Lepidus
Are in the field: a mighty strength they carry.

Caesar and Lepidus
Are on the battlefield: they have strong armies.

POMPEY
Where have you this? 'tis false.

MENAS
From Silvius, sir.

POMPEY
He dreams: I know they are in Rome together,

Looking for Antony. But all the charms of love,

Salt Cleopatra, soften thy waned lip!
Let witchcraft join with beauty, lust with both!

Tie up the libertine in a field of feasts,
Keep his brain fuming; Epicurean cooks
Sharpen with cloyless sauce his appetite;
That sleep and feeding may prorogue his honour
Even till a Lethe'd dulness!

Enter VARRIUS

How now, Varrius!

VARRIUS
This is most certain that I shall deliver:
Mark Antony is every hour in Rome
Expected: since he went from Egypt 'tis
A space for further travel.

POMPEY
I could have given less matter
A better ear. Menas, I did not think
This amorous surfeiter would have donn'd his helm
For such a petty war: his soldiership

Is twice the other twain: but let us rear
The higher our opinion, that our stirring

Can from the lap of Egypt's widow pluck
The ne'er-lust-wearied Antony.

MENAS
I cannot hope
Caesar and Antony shall well greet together:
His wife that's dead did trespasses to Caesar;
His brother warr'd upon him; although, I think,
Not moved by Antony.

Where did you hear this? It's false.

From Silvius, sir.

He is imagining it: I know they are in Rome together,
Looking for Antony. But all the attractive things about love,
Salty Cleopatra, soften your lips!
Let witchcraft combine with beauty, and lust with both!
Tie up the immoral man in a field of feasts,
Keep his brain confused; gourmet cooks
Sharpen his appetite with delicious sauces;
So that sleeping and eating may reduce his honor
To a forgetful dullness!

What's going on, Varrius?

I certainly will deliver this news:
Mark Antony is, at any time now,
Expected in Rome: since he left Egypt there is
A space for even more travel.

I could have given a shorter message
A more thorough listen. Menas, I did not think
This lover-boy would have put on his helmet
For such a little, unimportant war: his soldier's skills
Are twice the other two: but let us raise
Our opinion of ourselves even higher, that our causing trouble
Can separate from Egypt's queen
Antony, who never tires of lust.

I don't dare hope
That Caesar and Antony will get along well:
His dead wife did cause trouble to Caesar;
His brother fought him; although, I think,
Not encouraged by Antony.

POMPEY

I know not, Menas,
How lesser enmities may give way to greater.

Were't not that we stand up against them all,
'Twere pregnant they should square between
themselves;
For they have entertained cause enough
To draw their swords: but how the fear of us
May cement their divisions and bind up
The petty difference, we yet not know.
Be't as our gods will have't! It only stands

Our lives upon to use our strongest hands.
Come, Menas.

Exeunt

I don't know, Menas,
How smaller hatreds may be pushed aside for
larger.
If we weren't standing up against all of them,
It is likely they would attack each other;

Because they have given enough reasons
To pull out their swords: but how the fear of us
May bring them together and close up
The small differences, we don't know yet.
May it be according to the gods! It only makes
sense
To do the best we can in our lives.
Come along, Menas.

SCENE II. Rome. The house of LEPIDUS.

Enter DOMITIUS ENOBARBUS and LEPIDUS

LEPIDUS
Good Enobarbus, 'tis a worthy deed,
And shall become you well, to entreat your captain

To soft and gentle speech.

*My dear Enobarbus, it is a worthwhile action,
And will reflect well on you, to convince your captain
To speak softly and gently.*

DOMITIUS ENOBARBUS
I shall entreat him
To answer like himself: if Caesar move him,
Let Antony look over Caesar's head
And speak as loud as Mars. By Jupiter,
Were I the wearer of Antonius' beard,
I would not shave't to-day.

*I will convince him
To answer like himself: if Caesar motivates him,
Let Mark Antony look over Caesar's head
And speak as loudly as the god of war. By Jupiter,
If I had Antonius' beard,
I would not shave it today.*

LEPIDUS
Tis not a time
For private stomaching.

*This is not the time
For private feelings.*

DOMITIUS ENOBARBUS
Every time
Serves for the matter that is then born in't.

*Every time
Is suitable for what goes on during it.*

LEPIDUS
But small to greater matters must give way.

But small issues must be put aside for big deals.

DOMITIUS ENOBARBUS
Not if the small come first.

Not if the small ones come first.

LEPIDUS
Your speech is passion:
But, pray you, stir no embers up. Here comes

The noble Antony.

*Your speech is overly emotional:
But please, don't stir up things even more. Here comes
The noble Mark Antony.*

Enter MARK ANTONY and VENTIDIUS

DOMITIUS ENOBARBUS
And yonder, Caesar.

And over there, Caesar.

Enter OCTAVIUS CAESAR, MECAENAS, and AGRIPPA

MARK ANTONY
If we compose well here, to Parthia:
Hark, Ventidius.

If we do well here, we should go to Parthia:
Look, it's Venius.

OCTAVIUS CAESAR
I do not know,
Mecaenas; ask Agrippa.

I don't know;
Macaenas, ask Agrippa.

LEPIDUS
Noble friends,
That which combined us was most great, and let not

A leaner action rend us. What's amiss,
May it be gently heard: when we debate
Our trivial difference loud, we do commit
Murder in healing wounds: then, noble partners,

The rather, for I earnestly beseech,
Touch you the sourest points with sweetest terms,
Nor curstness grow to the matter.

My noble friends,
What has brought us together is very important,
and let's not
Respond inadequately. What is wrong,
May we speak calmly about it: when we debate
Our unimportant differences loudly, we end up
Worsening our healing wounds: then, noble
partners,
Instead, please,
I advice you to be diplomatic,
And not add to things with rudeness.

MARK ANTONY
'Tis spoken well.
Were we before our armies, and to fight.

I should do thus.

Well said.
If we were in front of our armies, and about to
fight.
I should act like this.

Flourish

OCTAVIUS CAESAR
Welcome to Rome.

Welcome to Rome.

MARK ANTONY
Thank you.

Thank you.

OCTAVIUS CAESAR
Sit.

Sit down.

MARK ANTONY
Sit, sir.

You sit down, sir.

OCTAVIUS CAESAR
Nay, then.

No, then.

MARK ANTONY
I learn, you take things ill which are not so,

Or being, concern you not.

I learn that you are offended by things which
aren't offensive,
Or are not your business.

OCTAVIUS CAESAR

I must be laugh'd at,
If, or for nothing or a little, I
Should say myself offended, and with you
Chiefly i' the world; more laugh'd at, that I should

Once name you derogately, when to sound your name
It not concern'd me.

MARK ANTONY
My being in Egypt, Caesar,
What was't to you?

OCTAVIUS CAESAR
No more than my residing here at Rome
Might be to you in Egypt: yet, if you there
Did practise on my state, your being in Egypt
Might be my question.

MARK ANTONY
How intend you, practised?

OCTAVIUS CAESAR
You may be pleased to catch at mine intent
By what did here befal me. Your wife and brother

Made wars upon me; and their contestation
Was theme for you, you were the word of war.

MARK ANTONY
You do mistake your business; my brother never
Did urge me in his act: I did inquire it;
And have my learning from some true reports,
That drew their swords with you. Did he not rather

Discredit my authority with yours;
And make the wars alike against my stomach,
Having alike your cause? Of this my letters

Before did satisfy you. If you'll patch a quarrel,
As matter whole you have not to make it with,
It must not be with this.

OCTAVIUS CAESAR
You praise yourself
By laying defects of judgment to me; but
You patch'd up your excuses.

MARK ANTONY
Not so, not so;
I know you could not lack, I am certain on't,

I must be laughed at,
If, for nothing or for a little, I
Would say I was offended, and since you
Are much more laughed at by others, that I ended
up
Once insulting you, when speaking your name
Does not concern me.

My time in Egypt, Caesar,
What did it matter to you?

No more than my living here at Rome
Might matter to you in Egypt: yet, if you there
Were on my state business, your being in Egypt
Might be my problem.

What do you mean by that?

You might figure out what I meant
By what happened to me here. Your wife and
brother
Fought against me; and their grab for power
Was about you as well, you were the motivation
for war.

You misunderstand; my brother never
Encouraged me in his actions: I did ask about it;
And have learned from some true reports,
That there was fighting against you. Didn't he,
instead,
Ignore my authority along with yours;
And fought no matter how I felt about it,
Treating us the same? You agreed with me in my
letters
Before this. If you end an argument,
And consider it ended, you cannot open it
All over again.

You make yourself look good
By putting all the bad judgment on me; but
You are nothing but excuses.

That's not true;
I know you could not be without, I am certain of it,

Very necessity of this thought, that I,
Your partner in the cause 'gainst which he fought,
Could not with graceful eyes attend those wars
Which fronted mine own peace. As for my wife,
I would you had her spirit in such another:
The third o' the world is yours; which with a snaffle

You may pace easy, but not such a wife.

DOMITIUS ENOBARBUS
Would we had all such wives, that the men might go

to wars with the women!

MARK ANTONY
So much uncurbable, her garboils, Caesar

Made out of her impatience, which not wanted
Shrewdness of policy too, I grieving grant
Did you too much disquiet: for that you must
But say, I could not help it.

OCTAVIUS CAESAR
I wrote to you
When rioting in Alexandria; you
Did pocket up my letters, and with taunts
Did gibe my missive out of audience.

MARK ANTONY
Sir,
He fell upon me ere admitted: then
Three kings I had newly feasted, and did want
Of what I was i' the morning: but next day
I told him of myself; which was as much
As to have ask'd him pardon. Let this fellow
Be nothing of our strife; if we contend,
Out of our question wipe him.

OCTAVIUS CAESAR
You have broken
The article of your oath; which you shall never
Have tongue to charge me with.

LEPIDUS
Soft, Caesar!

MARK ANTONY
No,
Lepidus, let him speak:
The honour is sacred which he talks on now,

A very necessary thought, that I,
Your partner in the cause he fought against,
Would not be able to calmly watch those wars
That harmed my own peace. As for my wife,
I wish you had her spirit in someone like her:
You rule over a third of the world; and you may have room
To walk comfortably, but not a wife like that.

If only we all had wives like that, so that men could go
to wars and fight alongside the women!

So much I could not hold back, her actions, Caesar
Made out of her impatience, which did not lack
Cleverness in leadership too, I must sadly admit
Caused you too much trouble: for that you can't
Say anything other than I could not help it.

I wrote to you
When there was rioting in Alexandria; you
Put away my letters, and with insults
Disregarded my messenger.

Sir
He came to me without permission: then
I had just feasted with three kings, and wasn't
Available that morning: but the next day
I told him about it myself; which was basically
Like apologizing. Let this man
Not be something to argue over; if we must,
We'll push him off the table of things to discuss.

You have broken
Your solemn promises; so you will never
Have a right to accuse me of anything.

Calm down, Caesar!

No,
Lepidus, let him talk:
The honor he is talking about now is sacred,

Supposing that I lack'd it. But, on, Caesar;
The article of my oath.

OCTAVIUS CAESAR
To lend me arms and aid when I required them;

The which you both denied.

MARK ANTONY
Neglected, rather;
And then when poison'd hours had bound me up
From mine own knowledge. As nearly as I may,
I'll play the penitent to you: but mine honesty
Shall not make poor my greatness, nor my power
Work without it. Truth is, that Fulvia,
To have me out of Egypt, made wars here;
For which myself, the ignorant motive, do

So far ask pardon as befits mine honour
To stoop in such a case.

LEPIDUS
'Tis noble spoken.

MECAENAS
If it might please you, to enforce no further
The griefs between ye: to forget them quite

Were to remember that the present need
Speaks to atone you.

LEPIDUS
Worthily spoken, Mecaenas.

DOMITIUS ENOBARBUS
Or, if you borrow one another's love for the
instant, you may, when you hear no more words of

Pompey, return it again: you shall have time to

wrangle in when you have nothing else to do.

MARK ANTONY
Thou art a soldier only: speak no more.

DOMITIUS ENOBARBUS
That truth should be silent I had almost forgot.

MARK ANTONY
You wrong this presence; therefore speak no more.

Which he thinks I don't have. But, go on, Caesar;
The promise you are referring to.

To lend me weapons and help when I needed them;
Which you both denied me.

No, it was just delayed;
And that was when I lost track of time
Before I was aware of it. As much as I can,
I'll make it up to you: but my honesty
Will not reduce my greatness, and my power
Won't work without it. The truth is, Fulvia,
To get me out of Egypt, made wars here;
For which I myself, the unintentional and unaware reason,
As as much forgiveness as is suitable for my honor
To humble myself in such a situation.

That is nobly said.

If you would be willing, to push no further
The problems between you: to forget them completely
Would be to remember that the current need
Is enough to make up for you.

Well and wisely said, Mecaenas.

Or, if you temporarily make peace for
now, you may, when you no longer have to deal with
Pompey, go back to your fighting: you will have time
to tussle when you have nothing else to do.

You are only a soldier: quiet.

Oh, sorry, I forgot that truth should be silent.

You are wrong in this case; so be quiet.

DOMITIUS ENOBARBUS
Go to, then; your considerate stone.

Get out, then; you considerate stone.

OCTAVIUS CAESAR
I do not much dislike the matter, but
The manner of his speech; for't cannot be
We shall remain in friendship, our conditions
So differing in their acts. Yet if I knew
What hoop should hold us stanch, from edge to edge

O' the world I would pursue it.

I do not actually dislike what he says, but
Instead how he says it; for it cannot be
That we shall stay friends, our conditions
So different in how we act. Yet if I knew
What connection could keep us together, from
every part
Of the world I would chase after it.

AGRIPPA
Give me leave, Caesar,--

Give me permission, Caesar --

OCTAVIUS CAESAR
Speak, Agrippa.

Go on, Agrippa.

AGRIPPA
Thou hast a sister by the mother's side,
Admired Octavia: great Mark Antony
Is now a widower.

You have a sister on your mother's side,
The admired Octavia: great Mark Antony
Is now a windowed.

OCTAVIUS CAESAR
Say not so, Agrippa:
If Cleopatra heard you, your reproof
Were well deserved of rashness.

Do not say that, Agrippa:
If Cleopatra heard you, your punishment
Would be well-deserved for your foolishness.

MARK ANTONY
I am not married, Caesar: let me hear
Agrippa further speak.

I am not married, Caesar: let me hear
Agrippa speak further.

AGRIPPA
To hold you in perpetual amity,
To make you brothers, and to knit your hearts

With an unslipping knot, take Antony
Octavia to his wife; whose beauty claims
No worse a husband than the best of men;
Whose virtue and whose general graces speak
That which none else can utter. By this marriage,
All little jealousies, which now seem great,
And all great fears, which now import their dangers,
Would then be nothing: truths would be tales,
Where now half tales be truths: her love to both

Would, each to other and all loves to both,
Draw after her. Pardon what I have spoke;

To keep you in constant agreement,
To make you brothers, and to tie your hearts
together
With a knot that will not slip, have Antony
Marry Octavia; she's beautiful enough
For the best of men to be her husband;
And her goodness and general gracefulness speak
Well of her. By this marriage,
All the little problems, which now seem big,
And all big fears, which come from their dangers,
Would then be nothing: facts would be stories,
Where now only partial facts are true: her love to
both
Would, each of them to each other,
Come together because of her. Forgive me for
speaking;

For 'tis a studied, not a present thought,

By duty ruminated.

MARK ANTONY
Will Caesar speak?

OCTAVIUS CAESAR
Not till he hears how Antony is touch'd
With what is spoke already.

MARK ANTONY
What power is in Agrippa,
If I would say, 'Agrippa, be it so,'
To make this good?

OCTAVIUS CAESAR
The power of Caesar, and
His power unto Octavia.

MARK ANTONY
May I never
To this good purpose, that so fairly shows,
Dream of impediment! Let me have thy hand:
Further this act of grace: and from this hour
The heart of brothers govern in our loves
And sway our great designs!

OCTAVIUS CAESAR
There is my hand.
A sister I bequeath you, whom no brother
Did ever love so dearly: let her live
To join our kingdoms and our hearts; and never
Fly off our loves again!

LEPIDUS
Happily, amen!

MARK ANTONY
I did not think to draw my sword 'gainst Pompey;
For he hath laid strange courtesies and great
Of late upon me: I must thank him only,
Lest my remembrance suffer ill report;

At heel of that, defy him.

LEPIDUS
Time calls upon's:
Of us must Pompey presently be sought,
Or else he seeks out us.

For it is something I have thought about, not a sudden idea,
And properly considered.

Does Caesar have anything to say?

Not until I hear how Antony is affected
By what is spoken already.

What power does Agrippa have,
If I were to say, 'Agrippa, make it so,'
To make this happen?

My own power, and
My power over Octavia.

May I never
To this good solution, that seems so reasonable,
Dream of preventing! Let me have your hand:
Continue this act of grace: and from now on
May the heart of brothers rule over our feelings
And affect our big plans!

Here is my hand.
I give you my sister, whom no brother
Ever loved so dearly: may she live
To join our kingdoms and our hearts; and never
Fight between us again!

May it be so!

I did not think to fight against Pompey;
For he has been very polite and given many favors
Recently: I must only thank him,
So that my gratefulness will not lose its reputation;
And then afterwards, go against him.

Time calls upon us:
We must go after Pompey soon,
Or else he will come after us.

MARK ANTONY
Where lies he?

Where is he camping?

OCTAVIUS CAESAR
About the mount Misenum.

Around Misenum Mountain.

MARK ANTONY
What is his strength by land?

How are his armies?

OCTAVIUS CAESAR
Great and increasing: but by sea
He is an absolute master.

Large, powerful, and increasing: but by sea
He rules absolutely.

MARK ANTONY
So is the fame.
Would we had spoke together! Haste we for it:

Yet, ere we put ourselves in arms, dispatch we
The business we have talk'd of.

That's what people say.
If only we had spoken together before! We must hurry:
But, before we put our armor on, we should go
And take care of the business we have been discussing.

OCTAVIUS CAESAR
With most gladness:
And do invite you to my sister's view,
Whither straight I'll lead you.

Gladly,
And I invite you to see my sister,
Where I'll lead you right away.

MARK ANTONY
Let us, Lepidus,
Not lack your company.

Let us, Lepidus,
Not be without you.

LEPIDUS
Noble Antony,
Not sickness should detain me.

Noble Mark Antony,
Nothing should prevent me.

Flourish. Exeunt OCTAVIUS CAESAR, MARK ANTONY, and LEPIDUS

MECAENAS
Welcome from Egypt, sir.

Welcome from Egypt, sir.

DOMITIUS ENOBARBUS
Half the heart of Caesar, worthy Mecaenas!
My honourable friend, Agrippa!

May you have half Caesar's heart, worthy
Mecaenas! My honorable friend, Agrippa!

AGRIPPA
Good Enobarbus!

Good to see you, Enobarbus!

MECAENAS
We have cause to be glad that matters are so well

digested. You stayed well by 't in Egypt.

We have reason to be glad that everything has turned out
so well. You had a good time in Egypt.

DOMITIUS ENOBARBUS
Ay, sir; we did sleep day out of countenance, and
made the night light with drinking.

*Yes, sir; we slept the day away, and
drank the night away too.*

MECAENAS
Eight wild-boars roasted whole at a breakfast, and
but twelve persons there; is this true?

*Eight wild boars were roasted whole for breakfast,
and only to feed twelve people; is this true?*

DOMITIUS ENOBARBUS
This was but as a fly by an eagle: we had much more
monstrous matter of feast, which worthily deserved
noting.

*Oh, that was nothing at all compared to some of
the feasting we did, it is very much worth
remembering.*

MECAENAS
She's a most triumphant lady, if report be square to her.

*She's an amazing lady, if reports are accurate
about her.*

DOMITIUS ENOBARBUS
When she first met Mark Antony, she pursed up
his heart, upon the river of Cydnus.

*When she first met Mark Antony, she captured
his heart, while sailing on the river Cydnus.*

AGRIPPA
There she appeared indeed; or my reporter devised
well for her.

*That is what I heard, or else my reporter lied
cleverly.*

DOMITIUS ENOBARBUS
I will tell you.
The barge she sat in, like a burnish'd throne,
Burn'd on the water: the poop was beaten gold;

Purple the sails, and so perfumed that

The winds were love-sick with them; the oars were
silver,
Which to the tune of flutes kept stroke, and made

The water which they beat to follow faster,
As amorous of their strokes. For her own person,
It beggar'd all description: she did lie
In her pavilion--cloth-of-gold of tissue--
O'er-picturing that Venus where we see
The fancy outwork nature: on each side her
Stood pretty dimpled boys, like smiling Cupids,

With divers-colour'd fans, whose wind did seem
To glow the delicate cheeks which they did cool,

And what they undid did.

*I will tell you.
The barge she sat in, like a shining throne,
Burned on the water: the upper deck was made of
beaten gold;
The sails were purple, and with so much perfume
that
The winds were dying of love; the oars were
silver,
Which were kept in time by the sound of flutes, and
made
The water which they beat splash faster,
As if passionate for the strokes. As for herself,
Any description would be inadequate: she lay
On her couch - with golden cloth -
Making someone think of Venus
In her beauty: on each side of her
Stood pretty young boys with dimples, like smiling
Cupids,
With fans of many colors, whose breezes seemed
To bring a glow to the delicate cheeks which they
cooled,
And undid what they did.*

AGRIPPA
O, rare for Antony!

Oh, lucky Antony!

DOMITIUS ENOBARBUS
Her gentlewomen, like the Nereides,
So many mermaids, tended her i' the eyes,
A strange invisible perfume hits the sense
Of the adjacent wharfs. The city cast
Her people out upon her; and Antony,
Enthroned i' the market-place, did sit alone,
Whistling to the air; which, but for vacancy,

Had gone to gaze on Cleopatra too,
And made a gap in nature.

AGRIPPA
Rare Egyptian!

DOMITIUS ENOBARBUS
Upon her landing, Antony sent to her,
Invited her to supper: she replied,
It should be better he became her guest;
Which she entreated: our courteous Antony,
Whom ne'er the word of 'No' woman heard speak,
Being barber'd ten times o'er, goes to the feast,
And for his ordinary pays his heart
For what his eyes eat only.

AGRIPPA
Royal wench!
She made great Caesar lay his sword to bed:
He plough'd her, and she cropp'd.

DOMITIUS ENOBARBUS
I saw her once
Hop forty paces through the public street;
And having lost her breath, she spoke, and panted,

That she did make defect perfection,
And, breathless, power breathe forth.

MECAENAS
Now Antony must leave her utterly.

DOMITIUS ENOBARBUS
Never; he will not:
Age cannot wither her, nor custom stale
Her infinite variety: other women cloy
The appetites they feed: but she makes hungry
Where most she satisfies.

MECAENAS
If beauty, wisdom, modesty, can settle

Her serving women, like the nymphs,
Or a group of mermaids, cared for her,
A strange invisible perfume drifts towards
Of the nearby piers. The city threw
Her people out to see her; and Antony,
Sitting in the marketplace, sat alone,
Whistling to the air; which, because of nothing else to do,
Had gone to look at Cleopatra too,
And made an empty space in nature.

Unique Egyptian!

When she landed, Antony sent a message to her,
Invited her to dinner: she replied,
It would be better if he became her guest;
Which she pleaded: our courteous Antony,
Who never says 'No' to a woman,
Being caught ten times over, goes to the feast,
And as a result pays his heart
Only for what his eyes eat.

Royal woman!
She made great Caesar put his sword away:
For the sake of love.

I saw her once
Run forty paces through the public street;
And once she lost her breath, she spoke, and panted,
That she made flaws into perfection,
And, breathless, breathed power.

Now Antony must leave her completely.

He never will:
Age cannot wrinkle her, or habit make dull
Her infinite variety: other women fill up
They appetites they feed: but she causes hunger
Where she satisfies most.

If beauty, wisdom, and quiet humility, can settle

The heart of Antony, Octavia is
A blessed lottery to him.

AGRIPPA
Let us go.
Good Enobarbus, make yourself my guest
Whilst you abide here.

DOMITIUS ENOBARBUS
Humbly, sir, I thank you.

Exeunt

Mark Antony's heart, Octavia is
A lucky win for him.

Let's go.
Dear Enobarbus, make yourself my guest
While you are staying here.

Thank you very much, sir.

SCENE III. The same. OCTAVIUS CAESAR's house.

Enter MARK ANTONY, OCTAVIUS CAESAR, OCTAVIA between them, and Attendants

MARK ANTONY
The world and my great office will sometimes
Divide me from your bosom.

The world and my high position will sometimes
Separate me from you.

OCTAVIA
All which time
Before the gods my knee shall bow my prayers
To them for you.

And that whole time
I shall bow to the gods and pray
To them for you.

MARK ANTONY
Good night, sir. My Octavia,
Read not my blemishes in the world's report:
Do not pay attention to my reputation according to the world,
I have not kept my square; but that to come

Shall all be done by the rule. Good night, dear lady.

Good night, sir.

Good night, sir. Octavia dear,
Read not my blemishes in the world's report:
Do not pay attention to my reputation according
to the world,
I have not been always responsible; but from now
on
Everything will be done according to the rules.
Goodnight, dear lady.
Goodnight, sir.

OCTAVIUS CAESAR
Good night.

Goodnight.

Exeunt OCTAVIUS CAESAR and OCTAVIA
Enter Soothsayer

MARK ANTONY
Now, sirrah; you do wish yourself in Egypt?

Now, man; you wish you were in Egypt?

Soothsayer
Would I had never come from thence, nor you Thither!

If only I had never come here from there, nor you
from there!

MARK ANTONY
If you can, your reason?

If you can tell me, what is your reason?

Soothsayer
I see it in
My motion, have it not in my tongue: but yet
Hie you to Egypt again.

I see it in
My mind, not yet able to say it: but still
Hurry back to Egypt again.

MARK ANTONY
Say to me,

Tell me,

Whose fortunes shall rise higher, Caesar's or mine?

Soothsayer
Caesar's.
Therefore, O Antony, stay not by his side:
Thy demon, that's thy spirit which keeps thee, is
Noble, courageous high, unmatchable,
Where Caesar's is not; but, near him, thy angel
Becomes a fear, as being o'erpower'd: therefore
Make space enough between you.

MARK ANTONY
Speak this no more.

Soothsayer
To none but thee; no more, but when to thee.
If thou dost play with him at any game,
Thou art sure to lose; and, of that natural luck,

He beats thee 'gainst the odds: thy lustre thickens,

When he shines by: I say again, thy spirit
Is all afraid to govern thee near him;
But, he away, 'tis noble.

MARK ANTONY
Get thee gone:
Say to Ventidius I would speak with him:

Exit Soothsayer

He shall to Parthia. Be it art or hap,

He hath spoken true: the very dice obey him;

And in our sports my better cunning faints
Under his chance: if we draw lots, he speeds;

His cocks do win the battle still of mine,
When it is all to nought; and his quails ever

Beat mine, inhoop'd, at odds. I will to Egypt:
And though I make this marriage for my peace,

I' the east my pleasure lies.

Enter VENTIDIUS

O, come, Ventidius,
You must to Parthia: your commission's ready;

Whose station in life will rise higher, Caesar's or mine?

Caesar's.
Therefore, Antony, do not stay by his side:
Your demon, that's your spirit which keeps you, is
Noble, brave, without match,
Where Caesar's is not; but, near him, your angel
Becomes a fear of being overpowered: therefore
Keep a good distance between you.

Say no more about this.

No one but you; no more, except when to you.
If you play with him at any game,
You are sure to lose; and, when it comes to natural luck,
He beats you against the odds: your luster thickens,
When he shines by: I say again, you spirit
Is all afraid to rule you near him;
But, when he is away, it is noble.

Go now:
Tell Ventidius I want to talk to him.

He will go to Parthia. Whether it is on purpose or by chance,
He has spoken the truth: the dice themselves obey him;
And in our sports my cleverness fails
Under his luck: if we draw lots, he gets the better one;
His fighting roosters win against mine,
Even when it is not important; and his quails always
Beat mine. I will go to Egypt:
And though I make this marriage for the sake of peace,
My pleasure lies in the east.

Come with me, Ventidius,
You must go to Parthia: your assignment's ready:

Follow me, and receive't.

Exeunt

Follow me, and receive it.

SCENE IV. The same. A street.

Enter LEPIDUS, MECAENAS, and AGRIPPA

LEPIDUS
Trouble yourselves no further: pray you, hasten

Your generals after.

Do not trouble yourselves any further: please, hurry
Your generals off to fight.

AGRIPPA
Sir, Mark Antony
Will e'en but kiss Octavia, and we'll follow.

Sir, Mark Antony
Could even just kiss Octavia, and we'll follow.

LEPIDUS
Till I shall see you in your soldier's dress,
Which will become you both, farewell.

Till I see you in your soldier's clothes,
Which will suit you both well, farewell.

MECAENAS
We shall,
As I conceive the journey, be at the Mount
Before you, Lepidus.

We will,
As I plan the journey, I will be at the mountain
Before you, Lepidus.

LEPIDUS
Your way is shorter;
My purposes do draw me much about:
You'll win two days upon me.

Your way is quicker;
My errands will make me have to wander a lot:
You'll beat me by two days.

MECAENAS AGRIPPA
Sir, good success!

Good luck, sir!

LEPIDUS
Farewell.

Farewell.

Exeunt

SCENE V. Alexandria. CLEOPATRA's palace.

Enter CLEOPATRA, CHARMIAN, IRAS, and ALEXAS

CLEOPATRA
Give me some music; music, moody food
Of us that trade in love.

Give me some music; music is that moody food
Of we that are in love.

Attendants
The music, ho!

Bring the music!

Enter MARDIAN

CLEOPATRA
Let it alone; let's to billiards: come, Charmian.

Leave it alone; let's play billiards: come,
Charmian.

CHARMIAN
My arm is sore; best play with Mardian.

My arm is sore; you should play with Mardian.

CLEOPATRA
As well a woman with an eunuch play'd
As with a woman. Come, you'll play with me, sir?

A woman can play with a eunuch
As well as with another woman. Come, you'll play
with me, sir?

MARDIAN
As well as I can, madam.

As well as I can, lady.

CLEOPATRA
And when good will is show'd, though't come
too short,
The actor may plead pardon. I'll none now:

Give me mine angle; we'll to the river: there,

My music playing far off, I will betray
Tawny-finn'd fishes; my bended hook shall pierce
Their slimy jaws; and, as I draw them up,
I'll think them every one an Antony,
And say 'Ah, ha! you're caught.'

And when good will is shown, even if it isn't
enough,
The actor may ask forgiveness. I won't do that
now:
Get me my fishing gear; we'll go to the river:
there,
My music playing far away, I will trick
the fishes; my bent hook will pierce
Their slimy jaws; and as I pull them up,
I'll think of each of them as an Antony,
And say 'Ah ha! You're caught.'

CHARMIAN
'Twas merry when
You wager'd on your angling; when your diver
Did hang a salt-fish on his hook, which he
With fervency drew up.

It was hilarious when
You bet on your fishing skills; when your diver
Hung a salted dead fish on his hook, which he
Worked very hard to pull up.

CLEOPATRA

That time,--O times!--
I laugh'd him out of patience; and that night

I laugh'd him into patience; and next morn,

Ere the ninth hour, I drunk him to his bed;
Then put my tires and mantles on him, whilst
I wore his sword Philippan.

Enter a Messenger

O, from Italy
Ram thou thy fruitful tidings in mine ears,
That long time have been barren.

Messenger
Madam, madam,--

CLEOPATRA
Antonius dead!--If thou say so, villain,
Thou kill'st thy mistress: but well and free,
If thou so yield him, there is gold, and here

My bluest veins to kiss; a hand that kings
Have lipp'd, and trembled kissing.

Messenger
First, madam, he is well.

CLEOPATRA
Why, there's more gold.
But, sirrah, mark, we use
To say the dead are well: bring it to that,
The gold I give thee will I melt and pour
Down thy ill-uttering throat.

Messenger
Good madam, hear me.

CLEOPATRA
Well, go to, I will;
But there's no goodness in thy face: if Antony
Be free and healthful,--so tart a favour
To trumpet such good tidings! If not well,
Thou shouldst come like a Fury crown'd with snakes,
Not like a formal man.

Messenger
Will't please you hear me?

That time, --oh, those times! --
I laughed him until he was impatient with me; and
that night
And I laughed him into patience again; and the
next morning
Before nine o'clock, I got him drunk to his bed;
Then put my clothes and crown on him, while
I wore his sword, named Philippan.

Oh, from Italy
Bring the good news to my ears
That for a long time have been like a desert.

Madam, madam,--

Oh no, Antony is dead! -- If you say so, villain,
You kill your lady: but well and free,
If you free him like that, here is some gold, and
here
My royal veins to kiss; a hand that kings
Have trembled to kiss.

First, madam, he is doing well.

Why, here's more gold.
But man, pay attention, we often
Say the dead are well: if that is the case,
I will melt the gold I give you and pour
Down your throat that tells bad news.

Good lady, please listen to me.

Well, go on, I will'
But there's no goodness in your face: if Antony
Is free and healthy, -- so important a favor
To announce such good news! If not well,
You should come like a Fury crowned with snakes,
Not like an official man.

Would you please listen to me?

CLEOPATRA
I have a mind to strike thee ere thou speak'st:
Yet if thou say Antony lives, is well,
Or friends with Caesar, or not captive to him,
I'll set thee in a shower of gold, and hail
Rich pearls upon thee.

I am thinking maybe I'll hit you before you speak:
But if you say Antony lives, is doing well,
Or friends with Caesar, or not his prisoner,
I'll put you in a shower of gold, and drop
Rich pearls on you.

Messenger
Madam, he's well.

Lady, he is doing well.

CLEOPATRA
Well said.

Good.

Messenger
And friends with Caesar.

And friends with Caesar.

CLEOPATRA
Thou'rt an honest man.

You are an honest man.

Messenger
Caesar and he are greater friends than ever.

Caesar and he are better friends than ever.

CLEOPATRA
Make thee a fortune from me.

Have a fortune from me.

Messenger
But yet, madam,--

But still, madam, --

CLEOPATRA
I do not like 'But yet,' it does allay
The good precedence; fie upon 'But yet'!
'But yet' is as a gaoler to bring forth
Some monstrous malefactor. Prithee, friend,
Pour out the pack of matter to mine ear,
The good and bad together: he's friends with Caesar:

In state of health thou say'st; and thou say'st free.

I do not like 'But still,' it ruins
What came before; out with 'But still'!
'But still" is like a jailor to bring out
Some evil monster. Please, friend,
Tell me the whole story,
The good and bad news together: he is friends
with Caesar:
You say healthy, and you say free.

Messenger
Free, madam! no; I made no such report:
He's bound unto Octavia.

Free, lady! No, I said no such thing:
He's tied to Octavia.

CLEOPATRA
For what good turn?

In what way?

Messenger
Madam, he's married to Octavia.

Madam, he married Octavia.

CLEOPATRA
The most infectious pestilence upon thee!

May you have the most terrible disease!

Strikes him down

Messenger
Good madam, patience.

Good lady, calm down.

CLEOPATRA
What say you? Hence,

What did you say? Go,

Strikes him again

Horrible villain! or I'll spurn thine eyes
Like balls before me; I'll unhair thy head:

*Horrible villain! Or I'll pull out your eyes
Like balls in front of me; I'll pull out your hair:*

She hales him up and down

Thou shalt be whipp'd with wire, and stew'd in brine,

You will be whipped with wire, and stewed in vinegar,

Smarting in lingering pickle.

With all the sting of pickles.

Messenger
Gracious madam,
I that do bring the news made not the match.

*Kind lady,
I bring the news, I had nothing to do with the match.*

CLEOPATRA
Say 'tis not so, a province I will give thee,
And make thy fortunes proud: the blow thou hadst
Shall make thy peace for moving me to rage;
And I will boot thee with what gift beside
Thy modesty can beg.

*Say it is not true, I will give you a province,
And I will make you rich: the blows you received
Will bring apology for bringing me to anger;
And I will send you away with better gifts
Than you can ask for.*

Messenger
He's married, madam.

He's married, lady.

CLEOPATRA
Rogue, thou hast lived too long.

Villain, you have lived too long.

Draws a knife

Messenger
Nay, then I'll run.
What mean you, madam? I have made no fault.

*No, then I'll run.
What do you mean, lady? I have done nothing wrong.*

Exit

CHARMIAN
Good madam, keep yourself within yourself:
The man is innocent.

*Good lady, stay calm and be reasonable:
The man is innocent.*

CLEOPATRA

Some innocents 'scape not the thunderbolt.

Melt Egypt into Nile! and kindly creatures

Turn all to serpents! Call the slave again:
Though I am mad, I will not bite him: call.

CHARMIAN
He is afeard to come.

CLEOPATRA
I will not hurt him.

Exit CHARMIAN

These hands do lack nobility, that they strike
A meaner than myself; since I myself
Have given myself the cause.

Re-enter CHARMIAN and Messenger

Come hither, sir.
Though it be honest, it is never good
To bring bad news: give to a gracious message
An host of tongues; but let ill tidings tell
Themselves when they be felt.

Messenger
I have done my duty.

CLEOPATRA
Is he married?
I cannot hate thee worser than I do,
If thou again say 'Yes.'

Messenger
He's married, madam.

CLEOPATRA
The gods confound thee! dost thou hold there still?

Messenger
Should I lie, madam?

CLEOPATRA
O, I would thou didst,
So half my Egypt were submerged and made
A cistern for scaled snakes! Go, get thee hence:
Hadst thou Narcissus in thy face, to me

Some innocent people do not escape the
thunderbolt.
Melt Egypt into the Nile! And may all gentle
creatures
Turn into snakes! Call the slave again:
Though I am insane with rage, I will not bite him:
call.

He is afraid to come.

I won't hurt him.

These hands are not acting nobly, for them to hit
Someone below me; since I myself
Have given myself the reason.

Come here, sir.
Though it is honest, it is never good
To bring bad news: give a happy message
A crowd of speakers; but let bad news tell
Itself when it is felt.

I have done my job.

Is he married?
I cannot hate you worse that I do,
If you say 'Yes' again.

He's married, lady.

May the gods ruin you! Are you sticking to that?

Should I lie, lady?

Oh, I wish you were lying,
So half my Egypt were underwater and made
A container for scaled snakes! Go, get out:
If you were the most handsome man in the world,
to me

Thou wouldst appear most ugly. He is married?

Messenger
I crave your highness' pardon.

CLEOPATRA
He is married?

Messenger
Take no offence that I would not offend you:
To punish me for what you make me do
Seems much unequal: he's married to Octavia.

Exit Messenger

CHARMIAN
Good your highness, patience.

CLEOPATRA
In praising Antony, I have dispraised Caesar.

CHARMIAN
Many times, madam.

CLEOPATRA
I am paid for't now.
Lead me from hence:
I faint: O Iras, Charmian! 'tis no matter.

Go to the fellow, good Alexas; bid him
Report the feature of Octavia, her years,
Her inclination, let him not leave out
The colour of her hair: bring me word quickly.

Exit ALEXAS

Let him for ever go:--let him not--Charmian,
Though he be painted one way like a Gorgon,

The other way's a Mars. Bid you Alexas

To MARDIAN
Bring me word how tall she is. Pity me, Charmian,

But do not speak to me. Lead me to my chamber.

Exeunt

You would appear incredibly ugly. He is married?

Please forgive me, your highness.

He's married?

*Take no offense that I do not want to offend you:
To punish me for what you force me to do
Seems very unfair: he's married to Octavia.*

Please, your highness, calm down.

While praising Antony, I have insulted Caesar.

Many times, lady.

*I am paying for it now.
Take me from here:
I feel faint: Oh, by Iras, Charmian! It is not important.
Go to that man, good Alexas; tell him
To tell the appearance of Octavia, her age,
Her personality, let him not leave out
The color of her hair: bring me answers quickly.*

*Let him go forever: --do not let him -- Charmian,
Even if one way he looks like a Gorgon [an ugly monster],
The other way is like Mars [handsome god of war]. Tell Alexas*

*Bring me answers about how tall she is. Pity me, Charmian,
But do not speak to me. Lead me to my room.*

SCENE VI. Near Misenum.

Flourish. Enter POMPEY and MENAS at one door, with drum and trumpet: at another, OCTAVIUS CAESAR, MARK ANTONY, LEPIDUS, DOMITIUS ENOBARBUS, MECAENAS, with Soldiers marching

POMPEY
Your hostages I have, so have you mine;
And we shall talk before we fight.

I have your hostages, and you have mine;
And we will talk before we fight.

OCTAVIUS CAESAR
Most meet
That first we come to words; and therefore have we

Our written purposes before us sent;
Which, if thou hast consider'd, let us know
If 'twill tie up thy discontented sword,

And carry back to Sicily much tall youth
That else must perish here.

It is appropriate
That we first come to words; and therefore we have
Written our negotiations;
Which if you have considered them, let us know
If it will make you put away your unsatisfied sword,
And take to Sicily many young men
That otherwise must die here.

POMPEY
To you all three,
The senators alone of this great world,
Chief factors for the gods, I do not know
Wherefore my father should revengers want,
Having a son and friends; since Julius Caesar,

Who at Philippi the good Brutus ghosted,
There saw you labouring for him. What was't
That moved pale Cassius to conspire; and what
Made the all-honour'd, honest Roman, Brutus,
With the arm'd rest, courtiers and beauteous freedom,

To drench the Capitol; but that they would
Have one man but a man? And that is it
Hath made me rig my navy; at whose burthen
The anger'd ocean foams; with which I meant
To scourge the ingratitude that despiteful Rome
Cast on my noble father.

To all three of you,
The only senators of this big world,
Speakers for the gods, I do not know
Why my father would want avengers,
Even after having a son and friends; since Julius Caesar,
Whom Brutus killed at Philippi,
And saw you working for him. What was it
That motivated pale Cassius to plot; and what
Made the honored, honest Roman, Brutus,
With enough soldiers, courtiers, and beautiful freedom,
To take over the Capitol; except that they wanted
One man to just be a man? And that is what
Has made me arm my navy; at whose command
The angered ocean foams; which is what I mean
To burn away the ingratitude that spiteful Rome
Threw at my noble father.

OCTAVIUS CAESAR
Take your time.

Take you time.

MARK ANTONY
Thou canst not fear us, Pompey, with thy sails;
We'll speak with thee at sea: at land, thou know'st
How much we do o'er-count thee.

You cannot fear us, Pompey, with your sails;
We'll speak with you at see; on land, you know
How much we outnumber you.

POMPEY
At land, indeed,
Thou dost o'er-count me of my father's house:
But, since the cuckoo builds not for himself,
Remain in't as thou mayst.

On land, I agree,
You outnumber me of my father's house;
But, since the cuckoo does not build for himself,
Remain in it as you like.

LEPIDUS
Be pleased to tell us--
For this is from the present--how you take
The offers we have sent you.

Please, tell us --
For this is about here and now -- how you feel
About the offers we have sent you.

OCTAVIUS CAESAR
There's the point.

That's the point.

MARK ANTONY
Which do not be entreated to, but weigh

What it is worth embraced.

Which you should not be convinced about, but
decide on your own
What is worth accepting.

OCTAVIUS CAESAR
And what may follow,
To try a larger fortune.

And what might happen after,
If you try for a bigger prize.

POMPEY
You have made me offer
Of Sicily, Sardinia; and I must
Rid all the sea of pirates; then, to send
Measures of wheat to Rome; this 'greed upon

To part with unhack'd edges, and bear back
Our targes undinted.

You have made me an offer
Of Sicily and Sardinia; and I must
Get rid of all the pirates; then, send
A certain amount of wheat to Rome: this agreed
upon
We do not fight, and take back
Our armies with no lives lost.

OCTAVIUS CAESAR MARK ANTONY LEPIDUS
That's our offer.

That is our offer.

POMPEY
Know, then,
I came before you here a man prepared
To take this offer: but Mark Antony
Put me to some impatience: though I lose
The praise of it by telling, you must know,

When Caesar and your brother were at blows,
Your mother came to Sicily and did find
Her welcome friendly.

You should know, then,
That I came to you here a man prepared
To make the deal: but Mark Antony
Upset me: though I lose
Some of the goodness by bragging about it, you
must know,
When Caesar and your brother were fighting,
Your mother came to Sicily and found
A friendly welcome.

MARK ANTONY
I have heard it, Pompey;
And am well studied for a liberal thanks
Which I do owe you.

I've heard it, Pompey;
And I have thought about the generous thanks
That I owe you.

POMPEY
Let me have your hand:
I did not think, sir, to have met you here.

Give me your hand:
I did not think, sir, that I would meet you here.

MARK ANTONY
The beds i' the east are soft; and thanks to you,
That call'd me timelier than my purpose hither;
For I have gain'd by 't.

The beds in the east are soft; and thanks to you,
That called me faster than my purpose here;
For I have gained by it.

OCTAVIUS CAESAR
Since I saw you last,
There is a change upon you.

Since I last saw you,
You have changed.

POMPEY
Well, I know not
What counts harsh fortune casts upon my face;
But in my bosom shall she never come,
To make my heart her vassal.

Well, I do not know
What bad luck does to my face;
But in my chest she will never come,
To make my heart her slave.

LEPIDUS
Well met here.

You are doing well here.

POMPEY
I hope so, Lepidus. Thus we are agreed:
I crave our composition may be written,
And seal'd between us.

I hope so, Lepidus. So we have agreed:
I would like our treaty to be written,
And sealed between us.

OCTAVIUS CAESAR
That's the next to do.

That's the next thing to do.

POMPEY
We'll feast each other ere we part; and let's

Draw lots who shall begin.

We'll treat each other to a feast before before we
separate; and let's
Draw straws who shall begin.

MARK ANTONY
That will I, Pompey.

I will, Pompey.

POMPEY
No, Antony, take the lot: but, first
Or last, your fine Egyptian cookery
Shall have the fame. I have heard that Julius Caesar

Grew fat with feasting there.

No, Antony, take your straw: but, first
Or last, your fine Egyptian cooking
Will be the most popular. I have heard that Julius
Caesar
Became fat with feasting there.

MARK ANTONY
You have heard much.

You have heard a lot.

POMPEY
I have fair meanings, sir.

I have honest reasons, sir.

MARK ANTONY
And fair words to them.

And pretty words about them.

POMPEY
Then so much have I heard:
And I have heard, Apollodorus carried--

I have heard so much:
And I have heard that Apollodorus carried --

DOMITIUS ENOBARBUS
No more of that: he did so.

Don't finish your sentence: he did.

POMPEY
What, I pray you?

What, please tell me?

DOMITIUS ENOBARBUS
A certain queen to Caesar in a mattress.

A certain queen to Caesar on a mattress.

POMPEY
I know thee now: how farest thou, soldier?

I recognize you now: how are you doing, soldier?

DOMITIUS ENOBARBUS
Well;
And well am like to do; for, I perceive,
Four feasts are toward.

Well;
And I am likely to continue doing well; for, I see
Four feasts are coming.

POMPEY
Let me shake thy hand;
I never hated thee: I have seen thee fight,
When I have envied thy behavior.

Let me shake your hand;
I never hated you: I have seen you fight,
When I have jealously admired your behavior.

DOMITIUS ENOBARBUS
Sir,
I never loved you much; but I ha' praised ye,

When you have well deserved ten times as much
As I have said you did.

Sir,
I never thought much of you; but I have praised you,
When you have deserved ten times more praise
As I said you did.

POMPEY
Enjoy thy plainness,
If nothing ill becomes thee.
Aboard my galley I invite you all:
Will you lead, lords?

Enjoy your simplicity,
If nothing bad happens to you.
I invite all of you onto my ship;
Will you lead, gentlemen?

OCTAVIUS CAESAR MARK ANTONY LEPIDUS
Show us the way, sir.

Sir, show us the way.

POMPEY
Come.

Come.

Exeunt all but MENAS and ENOBARBUS

MENAS

[Aside] Thy father, Pompey, would ne'er have made this treaty.--You and I have known, sir.

Your father, Pompey, would never have made this treaty. -- I have met you, I think.

DOMITIUS ENOBARBUS

At sea, I think.

At sea, I think.

MENAS

We have, sir.

We have, sir.

DOMITIUS ENOBARBUS

You have done well by water.

You have done well on the water.

MENAS

And you by land.

And you on land.

DOMITIUS ENOBARBUS

I will praise any man that will praise me; though it cannot be denied what I have done by land.

I will praise any man who will praise me; though it cannot be denied how well I have done by land.

MENAS

Nor what I have done by water.

Or how well I have done on water.

DOMITIUS ENOBARBUS

Yes, something you can deny for your own safety: you have been a great thief by sea.

Yes, something you can deny for your own safety: you have been a great thief on the sea.

MENAS

And you by land.

And you on land.

DOMITIUS ENOBARBUS

There I deny my land service. But give me your hand, Menas: if our eyes had authority, here they might take two thieves kissing.

I deny my land's service. But give me your hand, Menas: if our eyes saw accurately, here they might see two thieves kissing.

MENAS

All men's faces are true, whatsome'er their hands are.

All men's faces are honest, whatever their hands are.

DOMITIUS ENOBARBUS

But there is never a fair woman has a true face.

But no beautiful woman has an honest face.

MENAS

No slander; they steal hearts.

It's no lie; they steal hearts.

DOMITIUS ENOBARBUS

We came hither to fight with you.

We came here to fight with you.

MENAS

For my part, I am sorry it is turned to a drinking. Pompey doth this day laugh away his fortune.

As for me, I am sorry it has turned into drinking. Today Pompey laughs away his fortune.

DOMITIUS ENOBARBUS

If he do, sure, he cannot weep't back again.

If he does, surely, he cannot cry it back again.

MENAS

You've said, sir. We looked not for Mark Antony

here: pray you, is he married to Cleopatra?

*You've said it, sir. We did not expect to see Mark Antony
here: please tell me, is he married to Cleopatra?*

DOMITIUS ENOBARBUS

Caesar's sister is called Octavia.

Caesar's sister is named Octavia.

MENAS

True, sir; she was the wife of Caius Marcellus.

That's true, sir; she was the wife of Caius Marcellus.

DOMITIUS ENOBARBUS

But she is now the wife of Marcus Antonius.

But she is now married to Mark Antony.

MENAS

Pray ye, sir?

Is that really true, sir?

DOMITIUS ENOBARBUS

'Tis true.

It's true.

MENAS

Then is Caesar and he for ever knit together.

Then he and Caesar are connected forever.

DOMITIUS ENOBARBUS

If I were bound to divine of this unity, I would
not prophesy so.

*If I had to predict what would happen from now, I
would not think it will be that way.*

MENAS

I think the policy of that purpose made more in the
marriage than the love of the parties.

*I think this was more a political thing
than about any affection between the parties.*

DOMITIUS ENOBARBUS

I think so too. But you shall find, the band that
seems to tie their friendship together will be the
very strangler of their amity: Octavia is of a
holy, cold, and still conversation.

*I think so too. But, you will see, the knot that
seems to tie their friendship closer together will be
the very strangler of their friendship: Octavia is of
a religious, quiet, and still type.*

MENAS

Who would not have his wife so?

Who wouldn't want a wife like that?

DOMITIUS ENOBARBUS

Not he that himself is not so; which is Mark Antony.

He will to his Egyptian dish again: then shall the

sighs of Octavia blow the fire up in Caesar; and, as

*Not a man that is not like that himself; like Mark
Antony.
He will go back to his Egyptian love again: and
then the
sadness of Octavia will create anger in Caesar;
and, as*

I said before, that which is the strength of their

amity shall prove the immediate author of their

variance. Antony will use his affection where it is:

he married but his occasion here.

MENAS
And thus it may be. Come, sir, will you aboard?

I have a health for you.

DOMITIUS ENOBARBUS
I shall take it, sir: we have used our throats in Egypt.

MENAS
Come, let's away.

Exeunt

I said before, the very thing that is the strength of their
friendship will turn out to be the immediate reason for their
disagreement. Antony will use his affection where it is:
he only married an opportunity here.

And that may very well happen. Sir, will you come aboard?
I have a drink for you.

I will take it, sir: we have used our throats in Egypt.

Let's go, then.

SCENE VII. On board POMPEY's galley, off Misenum.

Music plays. Enter two or three Servants with a banquet

First Servant
Here they'll be, man. Some o' their plants are
ill-rooted already: the least wind i' the world
will blow them down.

Here they will be, man. Some of their plants are badly rooted already: the smallest wind in the world will blow them down.

Second Servant
Lepidus is high-coloured.

Lepidus is all red in the face.

First Servant
They have made him drink alms-drink.

They have made him drink strong liquor.

Second Servant
As they pinch one another by the disposition, he
cries out 'No more;' reconciles them to his
entreaty, and himself to the drink.

As they pinch each other as a joke, he yells, 'No more;' brings them to agree with his request, and himself to the drink.

First Servant
But it raises the greater war between him and
his discretion.

But it causes a bigger conflict between him and his good behavior.

Second Servant
Why, this is to have a name in great men's

fellowship: I had as lief have a reed that will do
me no service as a partisan I could not heave.

Why, this is what it's like to be known among great men,
I would be as willing to have a reed that would not be of any help to me as an ally I could not get rid of.

First Servant
To be called into a huge sphere, and not to be seen

to move in't, are the holes where eyes should be,
which pitifully disaster the cheeks.

To be brought into a huge circle, and not to be seen
to move in it, are the holes where eyes should be, which sadly ruin the cheeks.

A sennet sounded. Enter OCTAVIUS CAESAR, MARK ANTONY, LEPIDUS, POMPEY, AGRIPPA, MECAENAS, DOMITIUS ENOBARBUS, MENAS, with other captains

MARK ANTONY
[*To OCTAVIUS CAESAR*] Thus do they, sir: they take
the flow o' the Nile
By certain scales i' the pyramid; they know,

By the height, the lowness, or the mean, if dearth

That is how they do it, sir: they take
the flow of the Nile
By certain comparisons in to the pyramid; they know,
By the height, the lowness, or the average, if drought

Or foison follow: the higher Nilus swells,
The more it promises: as it ebbs, the seedsman
Upon the slime and ooze scatters his grain,
And shortly comes to harvest.

Or flood will follow: the higher the Nile swells,
The more it promises: as it flows out, the farmer
Scatters his seeds upon the slime,
And soon comes to a harvest.

LEPIDUS
You've strange serpents there.

There are strange snakes there.

MARK ANTONY
Ay, Lepidus.

Yes, Lepidus.

LEPIDUS
Your serpent of Egypt is bred now of your mud by the operation of your sun: so is your crocodile.

The snake of Egypt comes out of the mud because of the movement of the sun: so does the crocodile.

MARK ANTONY
They are so.

That is how it is, yes.

POMPEY
Sit,--and some wine! A health to Lepidus!

Sit, -- and some wine! A toast to Lepidus!

LEPIDUS
I am not so well as I should be, but I'll ne'er out.

I am not feeling as well as I should be, but I'll never quit.

DOMITIUS ENOBARBUS
Not till you have slept; I fear me you'll be in till then.

Not until you have slept: I'm afraid you'll keep going until then.

LEPIDUS
Nay, certainly, I have heard the Ptolemies' pyramises are very goodly things; without contradiction, I have heard that.

No, certainly, I have heard that Ptolemy's pyramids are very good things; without hearing otherwise, I have heard that.

MENAS
[Aside to POMPEY] Pompey, a word.

Pompey, I want to talk to you.

POMPEY
[Aside to MENAS] Say in mine ear:
what is't?

Whisper in my ear:
what is it?

MENAS
[Aside to POMPEY] Forsake thy seat, I do beseech thee, captain,
And hear me speak a word.

Get up from your seat, I request
your company, captain,
And listen to what I have to say.

POMPEY
[Aside to MENAS] Forbear me till anon.
This wine for Lepidus!

Leave me alone for a while.
This wine is for Lepidus!

LEPIDUS

What manner o' thing is your crocodile?

MARK ANTONY
It is shaped, sir, like itself; and it is as broad
as it hath breadth: it is just so high as it is,
and moves with its own organs: it lives by that
which nourisheth it; and the elements once out of
it, it transmigrates.

LEPIDUS
What colour is it of?

MARK ANTONY
Of it own colour too.

LEPIDUS
'Tis a strange serpent.

MARK ANTONY
'Tis so. And the tears of it are wet.

OCTAVIUS CAESAR
Will this description satisfy him?

MARK ANTONY
With the health that Pompey gives him, else he is a
very epicure.

POMPEY
[Aside to MENAS] Go hang, sir, hang! Tell me of
that? away!
Do as I bid you. Where's this cup I call'd for?

MENAS
[Aside to POMPEY] If for the sake of merit thou
wilt hear me,
Rise from thy stool.

POMPEY
[Aside to MENAS] I think thou'rt mad.
The matter?

Rises, and walks aside

MENAS
I have ever held my cap off to thy fortunes.

POMPEY
Thou hast served me with much faith.
What's else to say?

What is a crocodile, really?

*It is shaped like itself, sir; and it is as wide
as it has width: it is as tall as it is,
and moves with its limbs: it lives by
what it eats; and once it is done with something,
it excretes it.*

What color is it?

It is its own color, too.

That is a strange reptile.

Yes. And its tears are wet.

Will this description be enough for him?

*After the drink that Pompey gave him, or else he is
very picky.*

*Go away sir! Telling me about
that? away!
Do as I told you. Where is this cup I called for?*

*If out of necessity you
will listen to me,
Get out of your chair.*

*I think you are insane.
What's going on?*

I have always been in favor of your good luck.

*You have served me faithfully.
What else do you have to say?*

Be jolly, lords.

MARK ANTONY
These quick-sands, Lepidus,
Keep off them, for you sink.

MENAS
Wilt thou be lord of all the world?

POMPEY
What say'st thou?

MENAS
Wilt thou be lord of the whole world? That's twice.

POMPEY
How should that be?

MENAS
But entertain it,
And, though thou think me poor, I am the man

Will give thee all the world.

POMPEY
Hast thou drunk well?

MENAS
Now, Pompey, I have kept me from the cup.
Thou art, if thou darest be, the earthly Jove:
Whate'er the ocean pales, or sky inclips,

Is thine, if thou wilt ha't.

POMPEY
Show me which way.

MENAS
These three world-sharers, these competitors,
Are in thy vessel: let me cut the cable;
And, when we are put off, fall to their throats:
All there is thine.

POMPEY
Ah, this thou shouldst have done,
And not have spoke on't! In me 'tis villany;
In thee't had been good service. Thou must know,

'Tis not my profit that does lead mine honour;
Mine honour, it. Repent that e'er thy tongue

Be jolly, gentlemen.

You're standing on quicksand, Lepidus,
Be careful; you're sinking.

Do you want to rule the world?

What did you say?

Do you want to rule the world? That's twice.

How can that be?

Only give it a chance,
And, though you may think I am poor, I am the man
Who will give you the whole world.

Are you drunk?

Now, Pompey, I have stayed away from the wine.
You are, if you dare become, the god of Earth,
Whatever is within the ocean's bounds, or under the sky,
Is yours, if you will have it.

Show me how.

These three rulers, these competitors,
Are in your ship: let me cut the rope;
And, when we are floating away, kill them:
All of theirs will be yours.

Ah, you should have done it,
And not talked about it! In me it would be evil;
In you it would have been a good service. You must know,
It is not my profit that leads my honor;
But the other way around. Regret that you ever

Hath so betray'd thine act: being done unknown,

I should have found it afterwards well done;
But must condemn it now. Desist, and drink.

MENAS
[Aside] For this,
I'll never follow thy pall'd fortunes more.
Who seeks, and will not take when once 'tis offer'd,

Shall never find it more.

POMPEY
This health to Lepidus!

MARK ANTONY
Bear him ashore. I'll pledge it for him, Pompey.

DOMITIUS ENOBARBUS
Here's to thee, Menas!

MENAS
Enobarbus, welcome!

POMPEY
Fill till the cup be hid.

DOMITIUS ENOBARBUS
There's a strong fellow, Menas.

Pointing to the Attendant who carries off LEPIDUS

MENAS
Why?

DOMITIUS ENOBARBUS
A' bears the third part of the world, man; see'st not?

MENAS
The third part, then, is drunk: would it were all,
That it might go on wheels!

DOMITIUS ENOBARBUS
Drink thou; increase the reels.

MENAS
Come.

POMPEY
This is not yet an Alexandrian feast.

Betrayed yourself by speaking: if you had gone ahead
I would have afterwards found it well done;
But must forbid you now. Stop, and drink.

Because of this,
I'll never follow you again.
Someone who searches, and will not take once it is offered,
Shall never find it again.

This toast to Lepidus!

Carry him ashore. I'll toast it for him, Pompey.

Here's to you, Menas !

Welcome, Domitius Enobarbus!

Fill it until the cup brims over.

That's a strong fellow over there, Menas.

Why?

He carries a third of the world, man; don't you get it?

A third of it, then, is drunk: if only it all were,
So that it could go on wheels!

You drink; increase the reeling.

Come.

This is not yet a feast like in Alexandria.

MARK ANTONY
It ripens towards it. Strike the vessels, ho?
Here is to Caesar!

It comes near it. Hit the cups, yes?
Cheers for Caesar!

OCTAVIUS CAESAR
I could well forbear't.
It's monstrous labour, when I wash my brain,
And it grows fouler.

I could go without it.
It's a lot of work, when I wash my brain,
And it gets nastier.

MARK ANTONY
Be a child o' the time.

Enjoy the present moment.

OCTAVIUS CAESAR
Possess it, I'll make answer:
But I had rather fast from all four days
Than drink so much in one.

Own it, I'll answer:
But I would rather go without food for four days
Than drink so much in just one.

DOMITIUS ENOBARBUS
Ha, my brave emperor!

Ha, my brave emperor!

To MARK ANTONY

Shall we dance now the Egyptian Bacchanals,
And celebrate our drink?

Shall we now dance the Egyptian dances
And celebrate our drink?

POMPEY
Let's ha't, good soldier.

Let's have it, good soldier.

MARK ANTONY
Come, let's all take hands,
Till that the conquering wine hath steep'd our sense
In soft and delicate Lethe.

Come on, let's all take hands,
Until that powerful wine has bathed our senses
In the river of forgetfulness.

DOMITIUS ENOBARBUS
All take hands.
Make battery to our ears with the loud music:
The while I'll place you: then the boy shall sing;
The holding every man shall bear as loud
As his strong sides can volley.

Everyone join hands.
Assault our ears with the loud music:
And I'll put you together: then the boy will sing;
And every man shall sing aloud as loudly
As his strong body can manage.

Music plays. DOMITIUS ENOBARBUS places them hand in hand

THE SONG.
Come, thou monarch of the vine,
Plumpy Bacchus with pink eyne!
In thy fats our cares be drown'd,
With thy grapes our hairs be crown'd:
Cup us, till the world go round,
Cup us, till the world go round!

Come, you king of the grape vine,
Fat Bacchus with pink eyes!
In your fats our worries are drowned,
With your grapes our heads are crowned:
May we drink until the world goes round
May we drink until the world goes round!

OCTAVIUS CAESAR
What would you more? Pompey, good night.
Good brother,
Let me request you off: our graver business

Frowns at this levity. Gentle lords, let's part;

You see we have burnt our cheeks: strong Enobarb
Is weaker than the wine; and mine own tongue
Splits what it speaks: the wild disguise hath almost
Antick'd us all. What needs more words? Good night.
Good Antony, your hand.

POMPEY
I'll try you on the shore.

MARK ANTONY
And shall, sir; give's your hand.

POMPEY
O Antony,
You have my father's house,--But, what? we are friends.

Come, down into the boat.

DOMITIUS ENOBARBUS
Take heed you fall not.

Exeunt all but DOMITIUS ENOBARBUS and MENAS

Menas, I'll not on shore.

MENAS
No, to my cabin.
These drums! these trumpets, flutes! what!
Let Neptune hear we bid a loud farewell

To these great fellows: sound and be hang'd, sound out!

Sound a flourish, with drums

DOMITIUS ENOBARBUS
Ho! says a' There's my cap.

MENAS
Ho! Noble captain, come.

Exeunt

What more can you want? Pompey, good night.
Good brother,
Let me request that you come with me, our more serious business
Frowns at this playing around. Gentlemen, let's separate;
You see we have gone all flushed: strong Enobarb Is weaker than wine; and my own talking Is slurred: the wild disguise has almost made fools of us all. Need I say more? Good night. Antony, give me your hand.

I'll meet you on the shore.

I will, sir; give me your hand.

Oh, Antony,
You have my father's house, -- But what of it? We are friends.
Now let's go down into the boat.

Be careful that you don't fall.

Menas, I don't want to go on shore.

No, let's go to my cabin.
These drums! these trumpets, these flutes!
Let the god of the sea hear that we make a loud goodbye
To these great men: sound and then be quiet, sound out!

Hey, I say, there's my cap.

Hey! Noble captain, come with me.

ACT III

SCENE I. A plain in Syria.

Enter VENTIDIUS as it were in triumph, with SILIUS, and other Romans, Officers, and Soldiers; the dead body of PACORUS borne before him

VENTIDIUS
Now, darting Parthia, art thou struck; and now

Pleased fortune does of Marcus Crassus' death
Make me revenger. Bear the king's son's body
Before our army. Thy Pacorus, Orodes,
Pays this for Marcus Crassus.

SILIUS
Noble Ventidius,
Whilst yet with Parthian blood thy sword is warm,

The fugitive Parthians follow; spur through Media,

Mesopotamia, and the shelters whither
The routed fly: so thy grand captain Antony
Shall set thee on triumphant chariots and
Put garlands on thy head.

VENTIDIUS
O Silius, Silius,
I have done enough; a lower place, note well,
May make too great an act: for learn this, Silius;
Better to leave undone, than by our deed
Acquire too high a fame when him we serve's away.

Caesar and Antony have ever won
More in their officer than person: Sossius,
One of my place in Syria, his lieutenant,
For quick accumulation of renown,
Which he achieved by the minute, lost his favour.

Who does i' the wars more than his captain can

Becomes his captain's captain: and ambition,
The soldier's virtue, rather makes choice of loss,

Than gain which darkens him.

Now, quickly moving Parthia, you are hit; and now
Kind fortune has allowed me to avenge
Marcus Crassus' death. Carry the prince's body
In front of our army. Your Pacorus, Orodes,
Pays for the death of Marcus Crassus.

Noble Ventidius,
While your sword is still warm with Parthian blood,
The refugee Parthians follow; hurrying through Media,
Mesopotamia, and the shelters from where
The defeated escape: so your great leader Antony
Will put you on chariots of victory and
Put garlands on you head.

O Silius, Silius,
I have done enough; a lower position, observe,
May make an act too big: for learn this, Silius;
It is better to leave undone, than by our action
Become too famous when the one we serve is away.
Caesar and Antony have always won
More in their officers than by themselves: Sossius,
Whom I knew in Syria, his lieutenant,
Because of his quick getting of fame,
Which he managed by the minute, lost his good opinion.
The man who in the wars does more than his captain can
Becomes his captain's captain: and ambition,
The soldier's virtue, instead turns out to be more of a loss
Than a gain.

I could do more to do Antonius good,
But 'twould offend him; and in his offence
Should my performance perish.

SILIUS
Thou hast, Ventidius, that
Without the which a soldier, and his sword,
Grants scarce distinction. Thou wilt write to Antony!

VENTIDIUS
I'll humbly signify what in his name,
That magical word of war, we have effected;
How, with his banners and his well-paid ranks,
The ne'er-yet-beaten horse of Parthia
We have jaded out o' the field.

SILIUS
Where is he now?

VENTIDIUS
He purposeth to Athens: whither, with what haste

The weight we must convey with's will permit,
We shall appear before him. On there; pass along!

Exeunt

*I could do more to do Mark Antony good,
But it would offend him; and in his offense
I would come to ruin.*

*You have, Ventidius, that
Without having a soldier, and his sword,
Never get very far. You will write to Antony!*

*I'll humbly tell him what in his name,
That magical word of war, we have made happen;
How, with his flags and his well-paid soldiers,
The never-before-beaten Parthia
We have defeated.*

Where is he now?

*He has rushed off to Athens: which is where, with
whatever speed
The weight we have to take with us will allow,
We will appear in front of him. Go on there; pass
it along!*

SCENE II. Rome. An ante-chamber in OCTAVIUS CAESAR's house.

Enter AGRIPPA at one door, DOMITIUS ENOBARBUS at another

AGRIPPA
What, are the brothers parted?

What, have the brothers been separated?

DOMITIUS ENOBARBUS
They have dispatch'd with Pompey, he is gone;
The other three are sealing. Octavia weeps
To part from Rome; Caesar is sad; and Lepidus,

Since Pompey's feast, as Menas says, is troubled

With the green sickness.

They have finished with Pompey, he is gone;
The other three are recovering. Octavia cries
To be separated from Rome; Caesar is sad, and
Lepidus
Since Pompey's feast, as Menas says, has been
affected
With sickness.

AGRIPPA
'Tis a noble Lepidus.

He is a noble Lepidus.

DOMITIUS ENOBARBUS
A very fine one: O, how he loves Caesar!

A very fine one: oh, how he loves Caesar!

AGRIPPA
Nay, but how dearly he adores Mark Antony!

No, but how dearly he adores Mark Antony!

DOMITIUS ENOBARBUS
Caesar? Why, he's the Jupiter of men.

Caesar? Why, he's a leader god of men.

AGRIPPA
What's Antony? The god of Jupiter.

What is Antony, then? The god to a god.

DOMITIUS ENOBARBUS
Spake you of Caesar? How! the non-pareil!

Did you speak of Caesar? How! The example of
perfection!

AGRIPPA
O Antony! O thou Arabian bird!

Oh Antony! Oh you Arabian bird!

DOMITIUS ENOBARBUS
Would you praise Caesar, say 'Caesar:' go no further.

If you want to praise Caesar, just say 'Caesar:' go
no further.

AGRIPPA
Indeed, he plied them both with excellent praises.

Indeed, he flattered them both with excellent
praises.

DOMITIUS ENOBARBUS
But he loves Caesar best; yet he loves Antony:

But he loves Caesar best; still he loves Antony:

Ho! hearts, tongues, figures, scribes, bards, poets cannot
Think, speak, cast, write, sing, number, ho!
His love to Antony. But as for Caesar,
Kneel down, kneel down, and wonder.

AGRIPPA
Both he loves.

DOMITIUS ENOBARBUS
They are his shards, and he their beetle.

Trumpets within

So;
This is to horse. Adieu, noble Agrippa.

AGRIPPA
Good fortune, worthy soldier; and farewell.

Enter OCTAVIUS CAESAR, MARK ANTONY, LEPIDUS, and OCTAVIA

MARK ANTONY
No further, sir.

OCTAVIUS CAESAR
You take from me a great part of myself;
Use me well in 't. Sister, prove such a wife
As my thoughts make thee, and as my farthest band
Shall pass on thy approof. Most noble Antony,
Let not the piece of virtue, which is set

Betwixt us as the cement of our love,
To keep it builded, be the ram to batter

The fortress of it; for better might we

Have loved without this mean, if on both parts
This be not cherish'd.

MARK ANTONY
Make me not offended
In your distrust.

OCTAVIUS CAESAR
I have said.

MARK ANTONY
You shall not find,

Hey! Hearts, words, numbers, writers, singers, poets cannot
Think, speak, show, write, sing, number, hey!
His love for Antony. But as for Caesar,
Kneel down, kneel down, and be amazed.

He loves both.

They are his fragments, and he their beetle.

So;
I must go to my horse. Goodbye, noble Agrippa.

Good luck, worthy soldier, and farewell.

No farther, sir.

You take from me a large part of myself;
Take good care of her. Sister, be the kind of wife
As I think you can be, and as my farthest people
Can approve of. Most noble Antony,
Let not this example of goodness, which has been put
Between us as the cement of our love,
To keep it built up, turn out to be the battering ram
To bring down the fortress of it: for it would be better
To have loved without this reason, if on both parts
It is not respected and treasured.

Do not offend me
With your distrust.

I have spoken.

You will not find,

Though you be therein curious, the least cause

For what you seem to fear: so, the gods keep you,
And make the hearts of Romans serve your ends!
We will here part.

Though you seem to be worried about it, the least reason
For your fears: so, may the gods take care of you,
And may the hearts of Romans do as you want!
We will leave now.

OCTAVIUS CAESAR
Farewell, my dearest sister, fare thee well:
The elements be kind to thee, and make
Thy spirits all of comfort! fare thee well.

Goodbye, my dearest sister, farewell:
May the world be kind to you, and make
Your spirits full of comfort! Farewell.

OCTAVIA
My noble brother!

My noble brother!

MARK ANTONY
The April 's in her eyes: it is love's spring,
And these the showers to bring it on. Be cheerful.

April is in her eyes: it is love's spring,
And here is the rain to bring it on. Be cheerful.

OCTAVIA
Sir, look well to my husband's house; and--

Sir, take care of my husband's house; and --

OCTAVIUS CAESAR
What, Octavia?

Yes, Octavia?

OCTAVIA
I'll tell you in your ear.

I'll whisper in your ear.

MARK ANTONY
Her tongue will not obey her heart, nor can
Her heart inform her tongue,--the swan's down-feather,

That stands upon the swell at full of tide,
And neither way inclines.

Her words will not obey her heart, nor can
Her heart control her words, -- the swan's downy feather,
That stands upon the ocean wave,
And does not tilt either way.

DOMITIUS ENOBARBUS
[Aside to AGRIPPA] Will Caesar weep?

Is Caesar going to cry?

AGRIPPA
[Aside to DOMITIUS ENOBARBUS]
He has a cloud in 's face.

He has a cloud in his face.

DOMITIUS ENOBARBUS
[Aside to AGRIPPA] He were the worse for that,
were he a horse;
So is he, being a man.

He would be the worse for that,
if he were a horse;
And so he is, being a man.

AGRIPPA
[Aside to DOMITIUS ENOBARBUS] Why, Enobarbus,
When Antony found Julius Caesar dead,

Why, Enobarbus,
When Antony found Julius Caesar dead,

He cried almost to roaring; and he wept

When at Philippi he found Brutus slain.

DOMITIUS ENOBARBUS
[Aside to AGRIPPA] That year, indeed, he was
troubled with a rheum;
What willingly he did confound he wail'd,
Believe't, till I wept too.

OCTAVIUS CAESAR
No, sweet Octavia,
You shall hear from me still; the time shall not
Out-go my thinking on you.

MARK ANTONY
Come, sir, come;
I'll wrestle with you in my strength of love:
Look, here I have you; thus I let you go,
And give you to the gods.

OCTAVIUS CAESAR
Adieu; be happy!

LEPIDUS
Let all the number of the stars give light
To thy fair way!

OCTAVIUS CAESAR
Farewell, farewell!

Kisses OCTAVIA

MARK ANTONY
Farewell!

Trumpets sound. Exeunt

He cried until he was almost screaming; and he sobbed
When he found Brutus killed at Philippi.

That year, also, he was
troubled with a painful sickness:
What he willingly dealt with made him cry,
Believe it, until I cried too.

No, sweet Octavia,
You will still hear from me; the time will not
Stop me thinking of you.

Come on, sir, come on;
I'll wrestle with you over how strong my love is:
Look, here I have you; and like this I let you go,
And give you to the gods.

Goodbye; be happy!

May all of the stars give light
To your beautiful way!

Farewell, farewell!

Farewell!

SCENE III. Alexandria. CLEOPATRA's palace.

Enter CLEOPATRA, CHARMIAN, IRAS, and ALEXAS

CLEOPATRA
Where is the fellow?

Where is the man?

ALEXAS
Half afeard to come.

Half afraid to come.

CLEOPATRA
Go to, go to.

Go on, go on.

Enter the Messenger as before

Come hither, sir.

Come here, sir.

ALEXAS
Good majesty,
Herod of Jewry dare not look upon you

But when you are well pleased.

My good queen,
Even Herod of the Jews would not dare to look at you
Except when you are pleaed.

CLEOPATRA
That Herod's head
I'll have: but how, when Antony is gone
Through whom I might command it? Come thou near.

That traitor's head
I want: but how, when Antony is gone
Whom should I command it through? Come closer.

Messenger
Most gracious majesty,--

Most kind ruler,--

CLEOPATRA
Didst thou behold Octavia?

Did you see Octavia?

Messenger
Ay, dread queen.

Yes, fearsome queen.

CLEOPATRA
Where?

Where?

Messenger
Madam, in Rome;
I look'd her in the face, and saw her led
Between her brother and Mark Antony.

In Rome, Madam;
I looked her in the face, and saw her being led
Between her brother and Mark Antony.

CLEOPATRA
Is she as tall as me?

Is she as tall as I am?

Messenger
She is not, madam.

She isn't.

CLEOPATRA
Didst hear her speak? is she shrill-tongued or low?

Did you hear her speak? Does she have a high or low voice?

Messenger
Madam, I heard her speak; she is low-voiced.

Madam, I heard her speak; she has a low voice.

CLEOPATRA
That's not so good: he cannot like her long.

That is not good for her: he cannot like her long.

CHARMIAN
Like her! O Isis! 'tis impossible.

Like her! Oh Isis! That would be impossible.

CLEOPATRA
I think so, Charmian: dull of tongue, and dwarfish!

What majesty is in her gait? Remember,
If e'er thou look'dst on majesty.

I think so, Charmian: dull-sounding, and dwarfish!
What grace is their in her walk? Remember,
If you ever saw gracefulness.

Messenger
She creeps:
Her motion and her station are as one;
She shows a body rather than a life,
A statue than a breather.

She creeps:
Her motion and her position are the same;
She seems more like a body than a living person,
A statue rather than someone breathing.

CLEOPATRA
Is this certain?

Are you sure?

Messenger
Or I have no observance.

Or else I have no powers of observation.

CHARMIAN
Three in Egypt
Cannot make better note.

Three Egyptians
Could not be more observing.

CLEOPATRA
He's very knowing;
I do perceive't: there's nothing in her yet:
The fellow has good judgment.

He is very wise;
I can see it: there's no threat from her yet:
The man has good judgment.

CHARMIAN
Excellent.

Excellent.

CLEOPATRA
Guess at her years, I prithee.

Guess how old she is, please.

Messenger
Madam,
She was a widow,--

CLEOPATRA
Widow! Charmian, hark.

Messenger
And I do think she's thirty.

CLEOPATRA
Bear'st thou her face in mind? is't long or round?

Messenger
Round even to faultiness.

CLEOPATRA
For the most part, too, they are foolish that are so.

Her hair, what colour?

Messenger
Brown, madam: and her forehead
As low as she would wish it.

CLEOPATRA
There's gold for thee.
Thou must not take my former sharpness ill:

I will employ thee back again; I find thee
Most fit for business: go make thee ready;

Our letters are prepared.

Exit Messenger

CHARMIAN
A proper man.

CLEOPATRA
Indeed, he is so: I repent me much
That so I harried him. Why, methinks, by him,

This creature's no such thing.

CHARMIAN
Nothing, madam.

CLEOPATRA

Madam,
She was a widow,--

Widow! Charmian, pay attention.

And I think she's thirty.

Do you have her face in your mind's eye? Is it long or round?

A bit too round.

Most of the time, too, round-faced women are foolish.
What color is her hair?

Brown, madam: and her forehead
Is as low as it could be.

Here's some gold for you.
You must not be too offended by my earlier harshness.
I will hire you again; I find you
Very suitable fore business: go make yourself ready;
My letters have been prepared.

A good man.

Yes, he is: I very much regret
That I caused him so much trouble. Why, I think, through him,
This woman isn't much of anything.

Nothing, madam.

The man hath seen some majesty, and should know.

CHARMIAN
Hath he seen majesty? Isis else defend,
And serving you so long!

CLEOPATRA
I have one thing more to ask him yet, good Charmian:

But 'tis no matter; thou shalt bring him to me
Where I will write. All may be well enough.

CHARMIAN
I warrant you, madam.

Exeunt

This man has seen some grace and dignity, and should know.

*Has he seen grace and dignity? By Isis,
Of course he would have after serving you for so long!*

*I have one more thing to ask him still, good Charmian:
But it's no matter; you will bring him to me
Where I will be writing. All may turn out all right.*

I am sure it will, madam.

SCENE IV. Athens. A room in MARK ANTONY's house.

Enter MARK ANTONY and OCTAVIA

MARK ANTONY
Nay, nay, Octavia, not only that,--
That were excusable, that, and thousands more
Of semblable import,--but he hath waged
New wars 'gainst Pompey; made his will, and read it

To public ear:
Spoke scantly of me: when perforce he could not

But pay me terms of honour, cold and sickly

He vented them; most narrow measure lent me:

When the best hint was given him, he not took't,
Or did it from his teeth.

OCTAVIA
O my good lord,
Believe not all; or, if you must believe,
Stomach not all. A more unhappy lady,
If this division chance, ne'er stood between,

Praying for both parts:
The good gods me presently,
When I shall pray, 'O bless my lord and husband!'
Undo that prayer, by crying out as loud,
'O, bless my brother!' Husband win, win brother,

Prays, and destroys the prayer; no midway
'Twixt these extremes at all.

MARK ANTONY
Gentle Octavia,
Let your best love draw to that point, which seeks

Best to preserve it: if I lose mine honour,
I lose myself: better I were not yours
Than yours so branchless. But, as you requested,

Yourself shall go between 's: the mean time, lady,
I'll raise the preparation of a war

No, no, Octavia, not only that, --
That could be excused, that, and thousands more
Of similar importance, -- but he has fought
New wars against Pompey; made his will, and read it
For the public to hear:
Which hardly mentioned me: when it happened that he could not
Do anything but pay me terms of honor, cold and weak
He spoke them; he gave me the least honor he could:
When he was given a hint, he either didn't take it,
Or did through his teeth.

Oh, my good husband,
Do not believe it all; or, if you must believe,
Do not be upset by all. A more unhappy lady,
If this tears you apart, has never had to stand between,
Praying for both sides:
The good gods towards me soon,
When I will pray, 'Oh bless my honored husband!'
Undo that prayer, by crying out as loudly,
'Oh, bless my brother!' If the husband wins, or the brother wins
The prays destroy the prayers: there is no midway
Between those extremes at all.

Gentle Octavia,
Let your best love take you to that point, which searches
For how best to preserve it: if I lose my honor,
I lost myself: it would be better if I were not yours
Than yours so without branches. But, as you requested,
You will go between us: in the mean time, lady,
I'll begin preparing for war

Shall stain your brother: make your soonest haste;
So your desires are yours.

OCTAVIA
Thanks to my lord.
The Jove of power make me most weak, most weak,
Your reconciler! Wars 'twixt you twain would be
As if the world should cleave, and that slain men
Should solder up the rift.

MARK ANTONY
When it appears to you where this begins,
Turn your displeasure that way: for our faults
Can never be so equal, that your love
Can equally move with them. Provide your going;

Choose your own company, and command what cost
Your heart has mind to.

Exeunt

That will ruin your brother: hurry as best you can;
So you go with what you really want.

Thank you to my husband.
The god of power makes me weak, very weak,
Your diplomat! Wars between you two would be
As if the world would split, and killed men
Would fill up the crack.

When you come to a decision where this began,
Turn your blame that way: for our faults
Can never be equal enough to allow your love
To equally move between them. Prepare for leaving;
Choose your own company, and pay the price
Your heart decides upon.

SCENE V. The same. Another room.

Enter DOMITIUS ENOBARBUS and EROS, meeting

DOMITIUS ENOBARBUS
How now, friend Eros!

What's going on, my friend Eros?

EROS
There's strange news come, sir.

There is strange news now, sir.

DOMITIUS ENOBARBUS
What, man?

What?

EROS
Caesar and Lepidus have made wars upon Pompey.

Caesar and Lepidus have fought Pompey.

DOMITIUS ENOBARBUS
This is old: what is the success?

I knew that: what is the result?

EROS
Caesar, having made use of him in the wars 'gainst

Pompey, presently denied him rivality; would not let

him partake in the glory of the action: and not
resting here, accuses him of letters he had formerly

wrote to Pompey; upon his own appeal, seizes him: so
the poor third is up, till death enlarge his confine.

Caesar, having made use of him in the wars against
Pompey, soon after would not share with him, would not let
him take part in the glory of the action: and not resting here, accused him of betraying him in letters
written to Pompey: and put him in prison, so the poor third is out of the game, until death frees him.

DOMITIUS ENOBARBUS
Then, world, thou hast a pair of chaps, no more;
And throw between them all the food thou hast,
They'll grind the one the other. Where's Antony?

Then, world, you have a pair of gears, no more;
And throw between them all the food you have,
And they'll grind each other. Where's Antony?

EROS
He's walking in the garden--thus; and spurns
The rush that lies before him; cries, 'Fool Lepidus!'

And threats the throat of that his officer
That murder'd Pompey.

He's walking in the garden --- like this; and avoids
The work that is in front of him; yells, 'Fool Lepidus!'
And threatens the throat of the officer
That murdered Pompey.

DOMITIUS ENOBARBUS
Our great navy's rigg'd.

Our great navy is ready.

EROS
For Italy and Caesar. More, Domitius;
My lord desires you presently: my news
I might have told hereafter.

DOMITIUS ENOBARBUS
'Twill be naught:
But let it be. Bring me to Antony.

EROS
Come, sir.

Exeunt

For Italy and Caesar. More, Domitius;
My lord wants to talk to you: my news
I could have told afterwards.

It makes no difference:
But leave it alone. Take me to Antony.

Come, sir.

SCENE VI. Rome. OCTAVIUS CAESAR's house.

Enter OCTAVIUS CAESAR, AGRIPPA, and MECAENAS

OCTAVIUS CAESAR
Contemning Rome, he has done all this, and more,
In Alexandria: here's the manner of 't:
I' the market-place, on a tribunal silver'd,
Cleopatra and himself in chairs of gold
Were publicly enthroned: at the feet sat
Caesarion, whom they call my father's son,
And all the unlawful issue that their lust
Since then hath made between them. Unto her
He gave the stablishment of Egypt; made her
Of lower Syria, Cyprus, Lydia,
Absolute queen.

MECAENAS
This in the public eye?

OCTAVIUS CAESAR
I' the common show-place, where they exercise.
His sons he there proclaim'd the kings of kings:
Great Media, Parthia, and Armenia,
He gave to Alexander; to Ptolemy he assign'd
Syria, Cilicia, and Phoenicia: she
In the habiliments of the goddess Isis
That day appear'd; and oft before gave audience,

As 'tis reported, so.

MECAENAS
Let Rome be thus inform'd.

AGRIPPA
Who, queasy with his insolence
Already, will their good thoughts call from him.

OCTAVIUS CAESAR
The people know it; and have now received
His accusations.

AGRIPPA
Who does he accuse?

Condemning Rome, he has done all this, and more
In Alexandria: here is how it happened:
In the market-place, on a silver-plated stage,
Cleopatra and Mark Antony in gold chairs,
Were throned in public: at their feet sat
Caesarion, whom they call my father's son,
And all the illegitimate offspring that their lust
Has since been made betweem them. To her
He gave her the ruling of Egypt; made her
Of lower Syria, Cyprus, and Lydia
Absolute ruler.

This in front of the common people?

In the common show-place, where they exercise.
His sons he called the kings of kings there:
Great Media, Parthia, and Armenia
He gave to Alexander; to Ptolemy he gave
Syria, Cilicia, and Phoenicia, she
In the clothing of the goddess Isis
Appeared that day; and had often before received
visitors
As it is reported, in that way.

Let Rome be informed about this.

Who, uncomfortable with his rudeness
Already, will stop thinking good thoughts about
him.

The people know it; and now know about
His accusations.

Whom does he accuse?

OCTAVIUS CAESAR
Caesar: and that, having in Sicily
Sextus Pompeius spoil'd, we had not rated him
His part o' the isle: then does he say, he lent me
Some shipping unrestored: lastly, he frets

That Lepidus of the triumvirate
Should be deposed; and, being, that we detain

All his revenue.

*Caesar: that, having in Sicily
Ruined Sextus Pompeius, we have not given him
His part of the island: then he says he lent me
Some ships that were not returned: finally, he worries
That Lepidus of the three-way rule
Was deposed; and, this happening, that we hold back
All his money.*

AGRIPPA
Sir, this should be answer'd.

Sir, this should be answered.

OCTAVIUS CAESAR
'Tis done already, and the messenger gone.
I have told him, Lepidus was grown too cruel;

That he his high authority abused,
And did deserve his change: for what I have conquer'd,

I grant him part; but then, in his Armenia,
And other of his conquer'd kingdoms, I
Demand the like.

*It is done already, and the messenger gone.
I have told him that Lepidus had become too cruel;
And that he abused his high authority,
And deserved to be deposed: for what I have conquered
I gave him part; but then, in his Armenia
And his other conquered kingdoms, I
Demand the same treatment.*

MECAENAS
He'll never yield to that.

He'll never give in to that.

OCTAVIUS CAESAR
Nor must not then be yielded to in this.

And we must not give in to him.

Enter OCTAVIA with her train

OCTAVIA
Hail, Caesar, and my lord! hail, most dear Caesar!

Greetings, Caesar, and my brother! Greetings, most beloved Caesar!

OCTAVIUS CAESAR
That ever I should call thee castaway!

That I ever would have to call you a castaway!

OCTAVIA
You have not call'd me so, nor have you cause.

You have not called me that, and you have no reason to.

OCTAVIUS CAESAR
Why have you stol'n upon us thus! You come not

Like Caesar's sister: the wife of Antony
Should have an army for an usher, and
The neighs of horse to tell of her approach
Long ere she did appear; the trees by the way

*Why have you crept up on us like this? You do not come
Like Caesar's sister: Mark Antony's wife
Should have an army for a guide, and
The neighs of horses to reveal her coming
Long before she appears; the trees beside the path*

Should have borne men; and expectation fainted,

Longing for what it had not; nay, the dust
Should have ascended to the roof of heaven,
Raised by your populous troops: but you are come
A market-maid to Rome; and have prevented

The ostentation of our love, which, left unshown,
Is often left unloved; we should have met you
By sea and land; supplying every stage
With an augmented greeting.

OCTAVIA
Good my lord,
To come thus was I not constrain'd, but did
On my free will. My lord, Mark Antony,
Hearing that you prepared for war, acquainted
My grieved ear withal; whereon, I begg'd
His pardon for return.

OCTAVIUS CAESAR
Which soon he granted,
Being an obstruct 'tween his lust and him.

OCTAVIA
Do not say so, my lord.

OCTAVIUS CAESAR
I have eyes upon him,
And his affairs come to me on the wind.
Where is he now?

OCTAVIA
My lord, in Athens.

OCTAVIUS CAESAR
No, my most wronged sister; Cleopatra
Hath nodded him to her. He hath given his empire
Up to a whore; who now are levying
The kings o' the earth for war; he hath assembled
Bocchus, the king of Libya; Archelaus,
Of Cappadocia; Philadelphos, king
Of Paphlagonia; the Thracian king, Adallas;
King Malchus of Arabia; King of Pont;
Herod of Jewry; Mithridates, king
Of Comagene; Polemon and Amyntas,
The kings of Mede and Lycaonia,
With a more larger list of sceptres.

OCTAVIA

*Should have been full of men; and expectation
fainted,*
Longing for what it did not have; no, the dust
Should have climbed to the sky,
Raised by your many troops: but you have come
*Like an ordinary woman to Rome; and have
prevented*
A fancy show of our love, which, left not shown,
Is often not loved; we should have met you
By sea and land; adding to every stage
With an elaborate greeting.

My good lord,
I was not required to come this way, but did
Of my own free will. My lord, Mark Antony,
Hearing that you were preparing for war, let
Me know about it; after which, I begged
His pardon to let me return.

Which he quickly granted,
*Since you were an obstacle between his lust and
him.*

Don't say that, my lord.

I have spies watching him,
And I learn about his affairs.
Where is he now?

In Athens, my lord.

No, my much-wronged sister; Cleopatra
Has pulled him to her. He has given his empire
Up to a whore; who are now organizing
The kings of the Earth for war; he has assembled
Bocchus, the king of Libya; Archelaus,
Of Cappadocia; Philadelphos, king
Of Paphlagonia; the Thracian king, Adallas;
King Malchus of Arabia; King of Pont;
Herod of Jewry; Mithridates, king
Of Comagene; Polemon and Amyntas,
The kings of Mede and Lycaonia,
And there is an even larger list of rulers.

Ay me, most wretched,
That have my heart parted betwixt two friends
That do afflict each other!

OCTAVIUS CAESAR
Welcome hither:
Your letters did withhold our breaking forth;
Till we perceived, both how you were wrong led,

And we in negligent danger. Cheer your heart;

Be you not troubled with the time, which drives
O'er your content these strong necessities;
But let determined things to destiny
Hold unbewail'd their way. Welcome to Rome;

Nothing more dear to me. You are abused

Beyond the mark of thought: and the high gods,

To do you justice, make them ministers
Of us and those that love you. Best of comfort;
And ever welcome to us.

AGRIPPA
Welcome, lady.

MECAENAS
Welcome, dear madam.
Each heart in Rome does love and pity you:
Only the adulterous Antony, most large
In his abominations, turns you off;
And gives his potent regiment to a trull,
That noises it against us.

OCTAVIA
Is it so, sir?

OCTAVIUS CAESAR
Most certain. Sister, welcome: pray you,
Be ever known to patience: my dear'st sister!

Exeunt

Oh me, so unfortunate
To have my heart separated between two friends
That are having such problems with each other!

Welcome here:
Your letters did keep us from breaking apart;
Until we saw, both how how wrong you had been treated
And how much careless danger we were in. Cheer up;
Do not be troubled with the time, which drives
Over your contentment these things that must be;
But let decided things to destiny
Go on without being cried over. Welcome to Rome;
There is nothing more loved by me. You have been abused
Beyond what anyone could have thought; and the high gods,
To do you justice, make them servants
Of us and those that love you. Be comforted;
And always be welcome to us.

Welcome, lady.

Welcome, dear madam.
Every heart in Rome loves and pities you:
Only the unfaithful Antony, terrible
In his sins, pushes you away;
And gives his armies to a slut,
That pushes it against us.

Is that true, sir?

It is certain. Sister, welcome, please,
Be patient and happy, my dearest sister!

SCENE VII. Near Actium. MARK ANTONY's camp.

Enter CLEOPATRA and DOMITIUS ENOBARBUS

CLEOPATRA
I will be even with thee, doubt it not.

I will stay with you, do not doubt it.

DOMITIUS ENOBARBUS
But why, why, why?

But why, why, why?

CLEOPATRA
Thou hast forspoke my being in these wars,
And say'st it is not fit.

*You have spoken against my being in these wars,
And say it's not appropriate.*

DOMITIUS ENOBARBUS
Well, is it, is it?

Well, is it, is it?

CLEOPATRA
If not denounced against us, why should not we
Be there in person?

*If you are not against us, why should we not
Be there in person?*

DOMITIUS ENOBARBUS
Your presence needs must puzzle Antony;
Take from his heart, take from his brain, from his time,

What should not then be spared. He is already
Traduced for levity; and 'tis said in Rome

That Photinus an eunuch and your maids
Manage this war.

*Your presence distracts Antony;
Takes from his heart, takes from his brain, from his time,
Which he doesn't have to spare. He is already
Thought to be silly and foolish; and it is said in Rome
That Photinus, a eunuch, and your maids
Manage this war.*

CLEOPATRA
Sink Rome, and their tongues rot
That speak against us! A charge we bear i' the war,

And, as the president of my kingdom, will
Appear there for a man. Speak not against it:

I will not stay behind.

*Sink Rome, and may their tongues rot
That speak against us! We have a purpose in the war,
And, as the ruler of my kingdom, I will
Appear there instead of a man. Do not speak against it:
I will not stay behind.*

DOMITIUS ENOBARBUS
Nay, I have done.
Here comes the emperor.

*No, I'm done.
Here comes the emperor.*

Enter MARK ANTONY and CANIDIUS
MARK ANTONY
Is it not strange, Canidius,
That from Tarentum and Brundusium
He could so quickly cut the Ionian sea,
And take in Toryne? You have heard on't, sweet?

*Isn't it strange, Canidius,
That from Tarentum and Brundusium
He could so quickly cut the Ionian sea,
And take in Toryne? Have you heard about it, sweet?*

CLEOPATRA

Celerity is never more admired
Than by the negligent.

MARK ANTONY
A good rebuke,
Which might have well becomed the best of men,

To taunt at slackness. Canidius, we
Will fight with him by sea.

CLEOPATRA
By sea! what else?

CANIDIUS
Why will my lord do so?

MARK ANTONY
For that he dares us to't.

DOMITIUS ENOBARBUS
So hath my lord dared him to single fight.

CANIDIUS
Ay, and to wage this battle at Pharsalia.
Where Caesar fought with Pompey: but these offers,

Which serve not for his vantage, be shakes off;
And so should you.

DOMITIUS ENOBARBUS
Your ships are not well mann'd;
Your mariners are muleters, reapers, people
Ingross'd by swift impress; in Caesar's fleet
Are those that often have 'gainst Pompey fought:
Their ships are yare; yours, heavy: no disgrace

Shall fall you for refusing him at sea,
Being prepared for land.

MARK ANTONY
By sea, by sea.

DOMITIUS ENOBARBUS
Most worthy sir, you therein throw away
The absolute soldiership you have by land;
Distract your army, which doth most consist
Of war-mark'd footmen; leave unexecuted
Your own renowned knowledge; quite forego
The way which promises assurance; and
Give up yourself merely to chance and hazard,

Cleverness is never more admired
Than by the irresponsible.

A good criticism,
Which might have been good for even the best of
men,
To correct laziness. Canidius, we
Will fight with him by sea.

By sea! What else?

Why do that?

Because he dares us to it.

In the same way my lord has dared him to single
combat.

Yes, and to fight this battle at Pharsalia,
Where Caesar fought with Pompey: but these
offers,
Which do not serve his advantage, get shaken off;
And you should do the same.

Your ships are not well manned;
Your sailors are amateurs,
Not good fighters; in Caesar's fleet
Are those that have often fought against Pompey:
Their ships are light and fast; yours, heavy: no
disgrace
Will come to you for refusing at sea,
Being prepared for land.

By sea, by sea.

Good sir, by doing that you throw away
The absolute rule you have by land;
Distract your army, which mostly consists
Of experienced infantry; leave unused
Your own famous and admired knowledge; give up
The way that promises success; and
Give yourself up completely to blind luck,

From firm security.

Instead of security.

MARK ANTONY
I'll fight at sea.

I'll fight at sea.

CLEOPATRA
I have sixty sails, Caesar none better.

I have sixty ships, Caesar does not have any better.

MARK ANTONY
Our overplus of shipping will we burn;
And, with the rest full-mann'd, from the head of Actium
Beat the approaching Caesar. But if we fail,

We then can do't at land.

We will burn our extra cargo;
And, with the rest fully manned, from the head of Actium
We will defeat the approaching Caesar. But if we fail,
We can then do it on land.

Enter a Messenger

Thy business?

Your business?

Messenger
The news is true, my lord; he is descried;
Caesar has taken Toryne.

The news is true, my lord; he is victorious;
Caesar has taken Toryne.

MARK ANTONY
Can he be there in person? 'tis impossible;
Strange that power should be. Canidius,
Our nineteen legions thou shalt hold by land,
And our twelve thousand horse. We'll to our ship:

Away, my Thetis!

Can he be there in person? It's impossible;
How strange that power is. Canidius,
Our nineteen legions you will hold by land,
And our twelve thousand horses. We'll go to our ship:
Now let's go, my Thetis!

Enter a Soldier

How now, worthy soldier?

What's going on, worthy soldier?

Soldier
O noble emperor, do not fight by sea;
Trust not to rotten planks: do you misdoubt
This sword and these my wounds? Let the Egyptians

And the Phoenicians go a-ducking; we

Have used to conquer, standing on the earth,

And fighting foot to foot.

Oh noble emperor, do not fight by sea;
Do not trust rotten planks: do you doubt
My sword and my wounds' experience? Let the Egyptians
And the Phoenicians go swimming; we

Are used to conquering while standing on the ground,
And fighting foot to foot.

MARK ANTONY
Well, well: away!

Well, well; away!

Exeunt MARK ANTONY, QUEEN CLEOPATRA, and DOMITIUS ENOBARBUS

Soldier
By Hercules, I think I am i' the right.

By Hercules, I think I am right.

CANIDIUS
Soldier, thou art: but his whole action grows
Not in the power on't: so our leader's led,
And we are women's men.

Soldier, you are: but he is no longer
Motivated by logic: our leader is led,
And we are women's men.

Soldier
You keep by land
The legions and the horse whole, do you not?

You will keep on land
The legions and the cavalry, yes?

CANIDIUS
Marcus Octavius, Marcus Justeius,
Publicola, and Caelius, are for sea:
But we keep whole by land. This speed of Caesar's
Carries beyond belief.

Marcus Octavius, Marcus Justeius,
Publicola, and Caelius, are in favor of sea:
But we will stay on land. This speed of Caesar's
Is unbelievable.

Soldier
While he was yet in Rome,
His power went out in such distractions as
Beguiled all spies.

While he was still in Rome,
His power distracted and tricked
All the spies.

CANIDIUS
Who's his lieutenant, hear you?

Who is his lieutenant, do you know?

Soldier
They say, one Taurus.

They say he's named Taurus.

CANIDIUS
Well I know the man.

I know the man well.

Enter a Messenger

Messenger
The emperor calls Canidius.

The emperor calls Canidius.

CANIDIUS
With news the time's with labour, and throes forth,
Each minute, some.
Exeunt

With news the time is about work,
Every minute, some more.

SCENE VIII. A plain near Actium.

Enter OCTAVIUS CAESAR, and TAURUS, with his army, marching

OCTAVIUS CAESAR
Taurus!

Taurus!

TAURUS
My lord?

Sir?

OCTAVIUS CAESAR
Strike not by land; keep whole: provoke not battle,

Till we have done at sea. Do not exceed
The prescript of this scroll: our fortune lies
Upon this jump.

Do not fight on land; stand your ground: do not start a battle
Until we have finished at sea. Do not go beyond
This order: our whole fortune depends
Upon this move.

Exeunt

SCENE IX. Another part of the plain.

Enter MARK ANTONY and DOMITIUS ENOBARBUS

MARK ANTONY
Set we our squadrons on yond side o' the hill,
In eye of Caesar's battle; from which place
We may the number of the ships behold,
And so proceed accordingly.

Exeunt

Let us set our squadrons on this side of the hill,
Within view of Caesar's battle; from which
We may see the number of the ships,
And so proceed accordingly.

SCENE X. Another part of the plain.

CANIDIUS marcheth with his land army one way over the stage; and TAURUS, the lieutenant of OCTAVIUS CAESAR, the other way. After their going in, is heard the noise of a sea-fight Alarum. Enter DOMITIUS ENOBARBUS

DOMITIUS ENOBARBUS
Naught, naught all, naught! I can behold no longer:

The Antoniad, the Egyptian admiral,
With all their sixty, fly and turn the rudder:
To see't mine eyes are blasted.

Enter SCARUS

SCARUS
Gods and goddesses,
All the whole synod of them!

DOMITIUS ENOBARBUS
What's thy passion!

SCARUS
The greater cantle of the world is lost
With very ignorance; we have kiss'd away
Kingdoms and provinces.

DOMITIUS ENOBARBUS
How appears the fight?

SCARUS
On our side like the token'd pestilence,
Where death is sure. Yon ribaudred nag of Egypt,--

Whom leprosy o'ertake!--i' the midst o' the fight,

The breese upon her, like a cow in June,
Hoists sails and flies.

DOMITIUS ENOBARBUS
That I beheld:
Mine eyes did sicken at the sight, and could not
Endure a further view.

SCARUS
She once being loof'd,

All for nothing, nothing, nothing! I can't watch anymore;
The Antoniad, the Egyptian admiral,
With all their sixty ships, turn around and escape:
To see it burns my eyes.

Gods and goddesses,
The entire navy of them!

What's your opinion?

The larger wealth is lost
With ignorance; we have kissed away
Kingdoms and provinces.

How does the fight look?

On our side it is like a plague,
Where death is definite. Those weak soldiers of Egypt,--
May they have leprosy! -- In the middle of the fight,
The breeze upon her, like a cow in June,
Pulls up the sails and runs away.

I saw that:
My eyes sickened at the sight, and could not
Stand to watch any longer.

Once she had escaped,

The noble ruin of her magic, Antony,
Claps on his sea-wing, and, like a doting mallard,
Leaving the fight in height, flies after her:
I never saw an action of such shame;
Experience, manhood, honour, ne'er before
Did violate so itself.

DOMITIUS ENOBARBUS
Alack, alack!

Enter CANIDIUS

CANIDIUS
Our fortune on the sea is out of breath,
And sinks most lamentably. Had our general
Been what he knew himself, it had gone well:

O, he has given example for our flight,

Most grossly, by his own!

DOMITIUS ENOBARBUS
Ay, are you thereabouts?
Why, then, good night indeed.

CANIDIUS
Toward Peloponnesus are they fled.

SCARUS
'Tis easy to't; and there I will attend
What further comes.

CANIDIUS
To Caesar will I render
My legions and my horse: six kings already
Show me the way of yielding.

DOMITIUS ENOBARBUS
I'll yet follow
The wounded chance of Antony, though my reason

Sits in the wind against me.

Exeunt

The one who had ruined her, Antony,
Put up his sails, and, like a loving male duck,
Leaving the fight at its peak, sailed after her:
I never saw such a shameful action;
Experience, manhood, honor, never before
Violated itself so much.

Oh no, oh no!

We are out of luck on the sea,
And it sinks. If our general
Been himself and fought like he can, it would have
gone well:
Oh, he has given an example for our running
away,
Terribly, by his own!

Yes, are you around there?
Why, then, goodnight indeed.

They escaped towards Peloponnesus.

That is easily reached; and there I will deal with
What comes after.

To Caesar I will give
My armies and my horses: six kings already
Have shown me how to surrender.

I'll still follow
The unlikely way of Antony, even though it does
not

Seem reasonable to.

SCENE XI. Alexandria. CLEOPATRA's palace.

Enter MARK ANTONY with Attendants

MARK ANTONY
Hark! the land bids me tread no more upon't;
It is ashamed to bear me! Friends, come hither:
I am so lated in the world, that I
Have lost my way for ever: I have a ship
Laden with gold; take that, divide it; fly,
And make your peace with Caesar.

Listen! The land no longer wants me to walk upon it; It is ashamed to carry me! Friends, come here: I ham so ruined in the world, that I Have lost my way forever: I have a ship Full of gold; take it, share it; escape And make your peace with Caesar.

All
Fly! not we.

Run away! Not we.

MARK ANTONY
I have fled myself; and have instructed cowards
To run and show their shoulders. Friends, be gone;
I have myself resolved upon a course
Which has no need of you; be gone:
My treasure's in the harbour, take it. O,
I follow'd that I blush to look upon:
My very hairs do mutiny; for the white
Reprove the brown for rashness, and they them
For fear and doting. Friends, be gone: you shall

Have letters from me to some friends that will
Sweep your way for you. Pray you, look not sad,

Nor make replies of loathness: take the hint
Which my despair proclaims; let that be left
Which leaves itself: to the sea-side straightway:
I will possess you of that ship and treasure.
Leave me, I pray, a little: pray you now:
Nay, do so; for, indeed, I have lost command,
Therefore I pray you: I'll see you by and by.

I have run myself; and have told cowards To run and show their backs. Friends, be gone; I have decided on a plan Which does not need you; go: My treasure's in the harbor, take it. Oh, I followed what I blushed to look at: My very hairs rebel against me; for the white Scold the brown for riskiness, and they them For fear and caring too much. Friends, be gone; you will Have letters from me to some friends that will Make your pathway easier. Please, do not look sad, Or refuse any further: take the hint Which my despair announces; let that be left Which leaves itself: go to the sea: I will allow you to have that ship and treasure. Leave me, please, please now: No, do, because I have lost command, Therefore, please: I'll see you again.

Sits down
Enter CLEOPATRA led by CHARMIAN and IRAS; EROS following

EROS
Nay, gentle madam, to him, comfort him.

No, gentle madam, go to him, comfort him.

IRAS
Do, most dear queen.

Do, dearest queen.

CHARMIAN

Do! why: what else?

CLEOPATRA
Let me sit down. O Juno!

MARK ANTONY
No, no, no, no, no.

EROS
See you here, sir?

MARK ANTONY
O fie, fie, fie!

CHARMIAN
Madam!

IRAS
Madam, O good empress!

EROS
Sir, sir,--

MARK ANTONY
Yes, my lord, yes; he at Philippi kept
His sword e'en like a dancer; while I struck
The lean and wrinkled Cassius; and 'twas I
That the mad Brutus ended: he alone
Dealt on lieutenantry, and no practise had
In the brave squares of war: yet now--No matter.

CLEOPATRA
Ah, stand by.

EROS
The queen, my lord, the queen.

IRAS
Go to him, madam, speak to him:
He is unqualitied with very shame.

CLEOPATRA
Well then, sustain him: O!

EROS
Most noble sir, arise; the queen approaches:
Her head's declined, and death will seize her, but
Your comfort makes the rescue.

MARK ANTONY

Do! What else could you do?

Let me sit down. O Juno!

No, no, no, no, no.

Do you see, sir?

Oh damn, damn, damn!

Madam!

Madam, oh good empress!

Sir, sir,--

*Yes, my lord, yes: he kept at Philippi
His sword even like a dancer; while I hit
The lean and wrinkled Cassius, and it was me
Who killed insane Brutus: only he
Fought based on advice, and had no practice
In the brave field of war: but now -- Never mind.*

Ah, stay near.

The queen, sir, the queen.

*Go to him, lady, speak to him:
He is overcome with shame.*

Well then, help him: Oh!

*Noble sir, stand; the queen is coming:
Her head is sinking, and death will take her, but
Your comfort can save her.*

I have offended reputation,
A most unnoble swerving.

EROS
Sir, the queen.

MARK ANTONY
O, whither hast thou led me, Egypt? See,
How I convey my shame out of thine eyes
By looking back what I have left behind
'Stroy'd in dishonour.

CLEOPATRA
O my lord, my lord,
Forgive my fearful sails! I little thought
You would have follow'd.

MARK ANTONY
Egypt, thou knew'st too well
My heart was to thy rudder tied by the strings,
And thou shouldst tow me after: o'er my spirit
Thy full supremacy thou knew'st, and that
Thy beck might from the bidding of the gods
Command me.

CLEOPATRA
O, my pardon!

MARK ANTONY
Now I must
To the young man send humble treaties, dodge
And palter in the shifts of lowness; who
With half the bulk o' the world play'd as I pleased,
Making and marring fortunes. You did know
How much you were my conqueror; and that
My sword, made weak by my affection, would
Obey it on all cause.

CLEOPATRA
Pardon, pardon!

MARK ANTONY
Fall not a tear, I say; one of them rates
All that is won and lost: give me a kiss;
Even this repays me. We sent our schoolmaster;
Is he come back? Love, I am full of lead.
Some wine, within there, and our viands!
Fortune knows
We scorn her most when most she offers blows.
Exeunt

I have destroyed my reputation,
A very cowardly swerve.

Sir, the queen.

Oh, where have you led me, Egypt? See,
How I show my shame out of your eyes
By looking back on what I have left behind
Destroyed in dishonor.

Oh sir, sir,
Forgive my running away! I did not think
You were going to follow.

Egypt, you knew too well
That my heart was tied by strings to your rudder,
And you would tow me after: over my spirit
You know your absolute rule, and that
Your wants might from the orders of the gods
Command me.

Oh, forgive me!

Now I must
To the young man send humble messages, crawl
And kneel in lowness; I who
Played with half the world as I pleased,
Making and breaking fortunes. You knew
How much you had conquered me; and that
My sword, made weak by my love, would
Obey it no matter what.

I'm sorry, sorry!

Do not cry, I say; a single tear rates
All that is won and lost; give me a kiss;
Even that is repayment. We sent our teacher;
Has he come back? Love, my body is heavy.
Some wine and food!
Fortune knows
We dislike her most when she most gives us blows.

SCENE XII. Egypt. OCTAVIUS CAESAR's camp.

Enter OCTAVIUS CAESAR, DOLABELLA, THYREUS, with others

OCTAVIUS CAESAR
Let him appear that's come from Antony.
Know you him?

Let the messenger from Antony appear.
Do you know him?

DOLABELLA
Caesar, 'tis his schoolmaster:
An argument that he is pluck'd, when hither
He sends so poor a pinion off his wing,
Which had superfluous kings for messengers
Not many moons gone by.

Caesar, it is his teacher:
Which proves that he is desperate, when here
He sends such a common person,
When he had spare kings to use as messengers
Not many months ago.

Enter EUPHRONIUS, ambassador from MARK ANTONY

OCTAVIUS CAESAR
Approach, and speak.

Come closer, and speak.

EUPHRONIUS
Such as I am, I come from Antony:
I was of late as petty to his ends
As is the morn-dew on the myrtle-leaf
To his grand sea.

Such as I am, I come from Mark Antony:
I was recently as unimportant to his purposes
As the morning dew on a leaf
Is to the grand sea.

OCTAVIUS CAESAR
Be't so: declare thine office.

All right: state your business.

EUPHRONIUS
Lord of his fortunes he salutes thee, and
Requires to live in Egypt: which not granted,
He lessens his requests; and to thee sues
To let him breathe between the heavens and earth,
A private man in Athens: this for him.
Next, Cleopatra does confess thy greatness;
Submits her to thy might; and of thee craves
The circle of the Ptolemies for her heirs,
Now hazarded to thy grace.

He calls you the master of his fate, and
Asks to live in Egypt: which, if that is too much,
He is willing to have less; and begs you
To let him stay alive,
A private man in Athens. That settles him.
Next, Cleopatra admits to your greatness;
Submits to your power; and asks from you
Part of Egypt for her heirs,
Depending on your generosity.

OCTAVIUS CAESAR
For Antony,
I have no ears to his request. The queen
Of audience nor desire shall fail, so she
From Egypt drive her all-disgraced friend,
Or take his life there: this if she perform,
She shall not sue unheard. So to them both.

For Mark Antony,
I will not consider his request. The queen
Will not get to talk to me or get her request, unless
She chases her disgraced friend from Egypt,
Or kill him there: if she does this,
She can have what she wants. Tell them both.

EUPHRONIUS
Fortune pursue thee!

OCTAVIUS CAESAR
Bring him through the bands.

Exit EUPHRONIUS
To THYREUS

From Antony win Cleopatra: promise,
And in our name, what she requires; add more,
From thine invention, offers: women are not
In their best fortunes strong; but want will perjure
The ne'er touch'd vestal: try thy cunning, Thyreus;

Make thine own edict for thy pains, which we
Will answer as a law.

THYREUS
Caesar, I go.

OCTAVIUS CAESAR
Observe how Antony becomes his flaw,
And what thou think'st his very action speaks
In every power that moves.

THYREUS
Caesar, I shall.

Exeunt

Good luck to you!

Take him through the troops.

From Antony we will win Cleopatra: promise
And in our name, what she wants; add more,
Whatever offers you can think of: women are not
Strong even at the best of times; but need will ruin
Even the purest woman: try your cleverness,
Thyreus;
Make your own message in your work, which we
Will treat as law.

Caesar, I will go.

Look how Antony becomes his flaws,
And what you think his actions speak
In his very motion.

Caesar, I will.

SCENE XIII. Alexandria. CLEOPATRA's palace.

Enter CLEOPATRA, DOMITIUS ENOBARBUS, CHARMIAN, and IRAS

CLEOPATRA
What shall we do, Enobarbus?

What will we do, Enobarbus?

DOMITIUS ENOBARBUS
Think, and die.

Think, and die.

CLEOPATRA
Is Antony or we in fault for this?

Whose fault is it, Antony's or mine?

DOMITIUS ENOBARBUS
Antony only, that would make his will
Lord of his reason. What though you fled
From that great face of war, whose several ranges
Frighted each other? why should he follow?
The itch of his affection should not then
Have nick'd his captainship; at such a point,
When half to half the world opposed, he being

The meered question: 'twas a shame no less
Than was his loss, to course your flying flags,
And leave his navy gazing.

Only Antony's, who would make his emotions
Govern his reason. So what if you ran
From that battle, where several things
Made it frightening? Why should he follow?
His feelings of affection should not then
Damage his leadership; at such a point,
When the halves of the world were fighting one
another, he being
The one in question: it was a shame no less
Than it was his loss, to chase after your flags
And leave his navy confused.

CLEOPATRA
Prithee, peace.

Please, that's enough.

Enter MARK ANTONY with EUPHRONIUS, the Ambassador

MARK ANTONY
Is that his answer?

Is that his answer?

EUPHRONIUS
Ay, my lord.

Yes, my lord.

MARK ANTONY
The queen shall then have courtesy, so she
Will yield us up.

The queen will then have courtesy, if she
Gives me up.

EUPHRONIUS
He says so.

He says so.

MARK ANTONY
Let her know't.
To the boy Caesar send this grizzled head,

Let her know it.
To the boy Caesar send this old man's head,

And he will fill thy wishes to the brim
With principalities.

CLEOPATRA
That head, my lord?

MARK ANTONY
To him again: tell him he wears the rose
Of youth upon him; from which the world should note

Something particular: his coin, ships, legions,
May be a coward's; whose ministers would prevail
Under the service of a child as soon
As i' the command of Caesar: I dare him therefore

To lay his gay comparisons apart,
And answer me declined, sword against sword,
Ourselves alone. I'll write it: follow me.

Exeunt MARK ANTONY and EUPHRONIUS

DOMITIUS ENOBARBUS
[Aside] Yes, like enough, high-battled Caesar will
Unstate his happiness, and be staged to the show,
Against a sworder! I see men's judgments are
A parcel of their fortunes; and things outward

Do draw the inward quality after them,
To suffer all alike. That he should dream,
Knowing all measures, the full Caesar will
Answer his emptiness! Caesar, thou hast subdued

His judgment too.

Attendant
A messenger from CAESAR.

CLEOPATRA
What, no more ceremony? See, my women!
Against the blown rose may they stop their nose

That kneel'd unto the buds. Admit him, sir.

Exit Attendant

DOMITIUS ENOBARBUS
[Aside]
Mine honesty and I begin to square.
The loyalty well held to fools does make

And he will fill your wishes to the brim
With lands to rule over.

The head, sir?

To him again: tell him we has the blush
Of youth upon him; from which the world should notice
Something in particular: his money, ships, armies,
May be a coward's; whose advisers would win
While serving a child just as well
As they would under Caesar's: I therefore dare him
To put aside his friends,
And answer my challenge, sword against sword,
In single combat. I'll write it; follow me.

Yes, it is likely enough that victorious Caesar will
Put aside his happiness, and take part in the show,
Against a swordsman! I see men's judgments are
Just a part of their fortunes; and things on the outside
Affect things on the inside as well,
For all of them to suffer together. That he dreams,
Knowing all the factors, the full Caesar will
Respond to his emptiness! Caesar, you have conquered
Enter an Attendant

A messenger from Caesar.

What, no more fanfare? See, my women!
Against the blooming rose they may stick in their nose
That kneeled to the buds. Let him in, sir.

My honesty and myself begin to battle.
Being loyal to fools still makes

Our faith mere folly: yet he that can endure

To follow with allegiance a fall'n lord
Does conquer him that did his master conquer
And earns a place i' the story.

Enter THYREUS

CLEOPATRA
Caesar's will?

THYREUS
Hear it apart.

CLEOPATRA
None but friends: say boldly.

THYREUS
So, haply, are they friends to Antony.

DOMITIUS ENOBARBUS
He needs as many, sir, as Caesar has;
Or needs not us. If Caesar please, our master
Will leap to be his friend: for us, you know,
Whose he is we are, and that is, Caesar's.

THYREUS
So.
Thus then, thou most renown'd: Caesar entreats,

Not to consider in what case thou stand'st,
Further than he is Caesar.

CLEOPATRA
Go on: right royal.

THYREUS
He knows that you embrace not Antony
As you did love, but as you fear'd him.

CLEOPATRA
O!

THYREUS
The scars upon your honour, therefore, he
Does pity, as constrained blemishes,
Not as deserved.

CLEOPATRA
He is a god, and knows

Our loyalty into foolishness: yet he that can endure
To follow faithfully a fallen lord
Conquers the people his master conquered
And earns a place in the story.

What does Caesar want?

Listen in private.

Everyone here is a friend: speak openly.

So, by chance, they are friends of Antony.

He needs as many, sir, as Caesar has;
Or does not need us. If Caesar wishes, our master
Will leap to be his friend; for we, you know,
Will be friends with his friends, and that is,
Caesar's.

So.
In that way then, you famous and respected:
Caesar requests
Not to consider yourself standing
Further than he is Caesar.

Go on: so far very royal.

He knows that you stay with Antony
Not out of love, but out of fear.

Oh!

Therefore, the scars upon your honor, he
Pities as things that were forced on you,
Not as things you deserved.

He is a god, and knows

What is most right: mine honour was not yielded,
But conquer'd merely.

DOMITIUS ENOBARBUS
[Aside]
To be sure of that,
I will ask Antony. Sir, sir, thou art so leaky,
That we must leave thee to thy sinking, for
Thy dearest quit thee.

Exit

THYREUS
Shall I say to Caesar
What you require of him? for he partly begs
To be desired to give. It much would please him,
That of his fortunes you should make a staff
To lean upon: but it would warm his spirits,
To hear from me you had left Antony,
And put yourself under his shrowd,
The universal landlord.

CLEOPATRA
What's your name?

THYREUS
My name is Thyreus.

CLEOPATRA
Most kind messenger,
Say to great Caesar this: in deputation
I kiss his conquering hand: tell him, I am prompt
To lay my crown at 's feet, and there to kneel:
Tell him from his all-obeying breath I hear
The doom of Egypt.

THYREUS
'Tis your noblest course.
Wisdom and fortune combating together,
If that the former dare but what it can,
No chance may shake it. Give me grace to lay

My duty on your hand.

CLEOPATRA
Your Caesar's father oft,
When he hath mused of taking kingdoms in,
Bestow'd his lips on that unworthy place,
As it rain'd kisses.

What is right: my honor was not given up,
But only conquered.

To be sure of that,
I will ask Antony. Sir, sir, your ship is so leaky,
That we must leave you to your sinking, for
You nearest and dearest abandon you.

Should I say to Caesar
What you want from him? For he wishes
To be allowed to give. It would please him,
That of his wealth you would make a staff
To lean on: but it would warm his spirits,
To hear from me that you had left Mark Antony,
And put yourself under his protection,
The universal landlord.

What is your name?

My name is Thyreus.

Kindest messenger,
Say this to great Caesar: in gratitude
I kiss his conquering hand: tell him, I am ready
To lay my crown at his feet, and kneel there:
Tell him from his law-making words I hear
The fate of Egypt.

It is the best choice for you.
Wisdom and luck fighting together,
If wisdom dares only what it can do,
No chance may shake it. Give me permission to lay
My respect on your hand.

Your Caesar's father often,
When he had thoughts of taking kingdomes in,
Gifted his lips on that unworthy place,
As it rained kisses.

Re-enter MARK ANTONY and DOMITIUS ENOBARBUS

MARK ANTONY
Favours, by Jove that thunders!
What art thou, fellow?

Favors from Cleopatra, by Jove!
Who are you, fellow?

THYREUS
One that but performs
The bidding of the fullest man, and worthiest

To have command obey'd.

One who simply performs
The commands of the greatest man, and most
worthy
Of having himself obeyed.

DOMITIUS ENOBARBUS
[Aside]
You will be whipp'd.

You will be whipped.

MARK ANTONY
Approach, there! Ah, you kite! Now, gods and devils!
Authority melts from me: of late, when I cried 'Ho!'

Like boys unto a muss, kings would start forth,
And cry 'Your will?' Have you no ears?
am Antony yet.

Come, there! You hawk! Now, gods and devils!
Authority is melting from me: recently when I
yelled, 'Hey!"
Kings would rush forward, like boys to food,
And reply, 'What do you wish?' Do you have no
ears? I am still Antony.

Enter Attendants

Take hence this Jack, and whip him.

Take this guy and whip him.

DOMITIUS ENOBARBUS
[Aside]
'Tis better playing with a lion's whelp
Than with an old one dying.

It is better playing with a lion cub
Than with an old, dying one.

MARK ANTONY
Moon and stars!
Whip him. Were't twenty of the greatest tributaries

That do acknowledge Caesar, should I find them
So saucy with the hand of she here,--what's her name,
Since she was Cleopatra? Whip him, fellows,
Till, like a boy, you see him cringe his face,
And whine aloud for mercy: take him hence.

Moon and stars!
Whip him. Even if it were one of the twenty
greatest leaders
That bow before Caesar, if I found them
So saucy with the hand of this woman here
Whip him, men,
Till, like a boy, you see him wince and cringe,
And cry for mercy: take him from here.

THYREUS
Mark Antony!

Mark Antony!

MARK ANTONY
Tug him away: being whipp'd,
Bring him again: this Jack of Caesar's shall
Bear us an errand to him.

Pull him away: after he is whipped
Bring him back: this fool of Caesar's will
Take a message to him.

CLEOPATRA
O, is't come to this?

Oh, has it come to this?

MARK ANTONY
I found you as a morsel cold upon
Dead Caesar's trencher; nay, you were a fragment
Of Cneius Pompey's; besides what hotter hours,
Unregister'd in vulgar fame, you have
Luxuriously pick'd out: for, I am sure,
Though you can guess what temperance should be,
You know not what it is.

I found you like a cold morsel on
Dead Caesar's plate; no, you were a leftover
Of Cneius Pompey's, besides what slutty times
Not recorded in obscene reputation, you have
Luxuriously planned for: for, I am sure,
Though you can guess what self-control should be,
You don't know what it is.

CLEOPATRA
Wherefore is this?

Why are you doing this?

MARK ANTONY
To let a fellow that will take rewards
And say 'God quit you!' be familiar with
My playfellow, your hand; this kingly seal
And plighter of high hearts! O, that I were
Upon the hill of Basan, to outroar
The horned herd! for I have savage cause;
And to proclaim it civilly, were like
A halter'd neck which does the hangman thank
For being yare about him.

To let a man that will take rewards
And say, 'God quit you!' get to cozy up to
My playmate, your hand; this king's seal
And ruiner of hearts! Oh, if only I were
Upon the hill of Basan, to roar louder
Than the stags! For I have vicious reasons;
And to say it politely would be like
A noosed neck which the hanged man thanks
For being tight around him.

Re-enter Attendants with THYREUS

Is he whipp'd?

Has he been whipped?

First Attendant
Soundly, my lord.

Thoroughly, my lord.

MARK ANTONY
Cried he? and begg'd a' pardon?

Did he cry and beg forgiveness?

First Attendant
He did ask favour.

He did.

MARK ANTONY
If that thy father live, let him repent
Thou wast not made his daughter; and be thou sorry
To follow Caesar in his triumph, since
Thou hast been whipp'd for following him: henceforth

The white hand of a lady fever thee,
Shake thou to look on 't. Get thee back to Caesar,

Tell him thy entertainment: look, thou say

If your father lives, let him regret
You were not born his daughter; and be sorry
To follow Caesar in his victory, since
You have been whipped for following him: from
now on
May the hand of a lady make you feel ill,
And may you shiver to look at it. Get back to
Caesar,
Tell him how you have been treated: looking, you
say

He makes me angry with him; for he seems
Proud and disdainful, harping on what I am,
Not what he knew I was: he makes me angry;
And at this time most easy 'tis to do't,
When my good stars, that were my former guides,
Have empty left their orbs, and shot their fires
Into the abysm of hell. If he mislike
My speech and what is done, tell him he has

Hipparchus, my enfranched bondman, whom
He may at pleasure whip, or hang, or torture,
As he shall like, to quit me: urge it thou:
Hence with thy stripes, begone!

Exit THYREUS

CLEOPATRA
Have you done yet?

MARK ANTONY
Alack, our terrene moon
Is now eclipsed; and it portends alone
The fall of Antony!

CLEOPATRA
I must stay his time.

MARK ANTONY
To flatter Caesar, would you mingle eyes
With one that ties his points?

CLEOPATRA
Not know me yet?

MARK ANTONY
Cold-hearted toward me?

CLEOPATRA
Ah, dear, if I be so,
From my cold heart let heaven engender hail,
And poison it in the source; and the first stone

Drop in my neck: as it determines, so
Dissolve my life! The next Caesarion smite!

Till by degrees the memory of my womb,
Together with my brave Egyptians all,
By the discandying of this pelleted storm,
Lie graveless, till the flies and gnats of Nile
Have buried them for prey!

He makes me angry with him; for he seems
Proud and cold, going on about what I am,
Not what he knew I was: he makes me angry;
And at this time it is very easy to do it,
When my good stars, that used to guide me,
Have left their spaces empty, and shot their fires
Into the depths of hell. If he dislikes
My speech and what has been done, tell him he
has
Hipparchus, my slave, whom
He may whip, or hang, or torture
As he likes, to have revenge on me: urge him on:
Go away, with your whip wounds, get out!

Are you done yet?

Oh no, our earthly moon
Has been eclipsed; and it predicts nothing but
The fall of Mark Antony!

I must stay with him until his end.

To flatter Caesar, would you make eyes
At someone who serves him?

Don't you know me yet?

Cold-hearted toward me?

Oh, my dear, if I am,
May Heaven make hail from my cold heart,
And poison it from the source; and may the first
hailstone
Drop onto me, and then
Kill me! And may the next kill a follower of
Caesar!
Until little by little the memory of my womb,
Together with all my brave Egyptians,
By the destruction of this storm,
Lie unburied, until the flies and gnats of the Nile
Have buried them as food!

MARK ANTONY
I am satisfied.
Caesar sits down in Alexandria; where
I will oppose his fate. Our force by land
Hath nobly held; our sever'd navy too
Have knit again, and fleet, threatening most sea-like.

Where hast thou been, my heart? Dost thou hear, lady?

If from the field I shall return once more
To kiss these lips, I will appear in blood;
I and my sword will earn our chronicle:
There's hope in't yet.

CLEOPATRA
That's my brave lord!

MARK ANTONY
I will be treble-sinew'd, hearted, breathed,
And fight maliciously: for when mine hours
Were nice and lucky, men did ransom lives
Of me for jests; but now I'll set my teeth,
And send to darkness all that stop me. Come,
Let's have one other gaudy night: call to me
All my sad captains; fill our bowls once more;
Let's mock the midnight bell.

CLEOPATRA
It is my birth-day:
I had thought to have held it poor: but, since my lord

Is Antony again, I will be Cleopatra.

MARK ANTONY
We will yet do well.

CLEOPATRA
Call all his noble captains to my lord.

MARK ANTONY
Do so, we'll speak to them; and to-night I'll force
The wine peep through their scars. Come on, my queen;
There's sap in't yet. The next time I do fight,
I'll make death love me; for I will contend
Even with his pestilent scythe.

Exeunt all but DOMITIUS ENOBARBUS

DOMITIUS ENOBARBUS

I am satisfied.
Caesar sits in Alexandria; where
I will resist him. Our force by land
Has done well; our split navy too
Has come together again, and are threatening force.
Where have you been, my heart? Do you hear, lady?
If from the field I will return once more
To kiss these lips, I will appear in blood;
I and my sword will earn our place in history:
There's hope in it yet.

That's my brave lord!

I will have my muscles, heart, and breath,
And fight viciously: for when my hours
Were accurate and lucky, men fought
Against me for fun; but now I'll grit my teeth,
And destroy all that stoop me. Come,
Let's have one more night of fun: call to me
All my sad captains; fill our cups once more;
Let us drink away the night.

To day is my birthday;
I had thought it would be a sad one: but, since my lord
Is Mark Antony again, I will be Cleopatra.

We can still do well.

Call all his noble captains to my lord.

Do so, we'll talk to them; and tonight I'll force
The wine show through their scars. Come on, my queen;
There's hope still. The next time I fight,
I'll make death love me; for I will struggle against
Even his diseased scythe.

Now he'll outstare the lightning. To be furious,
Is to be frighted out of fear; and in that mood
The dove will peck the estridge; and I see still,
A diminution in our captain's brain
Restores his heart: when valour preys on reason,

It eats the sword it fights with. I will seek
Some way to leave him.

Exit

Now he'll be reckless. To be furious,
Is to be frightened out of fear; and in that mood
The dove will peck the hawk; and I still see,
A reduction in our captain's brain
Restores his heart: when courage overcomes
intelligence,
It eats the sword it fights with. I will try to find
Some way to leave him.

ACT IV

SCENE I. Before Alexandria. OCTAVIUS CAESAR's camp.

Enter OCTAVIUS CAESAR, AGRIPPA, and MECAENAS, with his Army; OCTAVIUS CAESAR reading a letter

OCTAVIUS CAESAR
He calls me boy; and chides, as he had power

To beat me out of Egypt; my messenger
He hath whipp'd with rods;
dares me to personal combat,
Caesar to Antony: let the old ruffian know
I have many other ways to die; meantime
Laugh at his challenge.

MECAENAS
Caesar must think,
When one so great begins to rage, he's hunted
Even to falling. Give him no breath, but now
Make boot of his distraction: never anger
Made good guard for itself.

OCTAVIUS CAESAR
Let our best heads
Know, that to-morrow the last of many battles
We mean to fight: within our files there are,
Of those that served Mark Antony but late,
Enough to fetch him in. See it done:
And feast the army; we have store to do't,

And they have earn'd the waste. Poor Antony!

Exeunt

He calls me a boy; and scolds, as if he had the power
To chase me out of Egypt; my messenger
He has whipped with sticks;
dares me to single combat,
Caesar to Antony: let the old scoundrel know
I have plenty of other ways to die; meanwhile
I laugh at his challenge.

Caesar must think,
When such a great man begins to rage, he is
Very close to falling. Give him no breath, but now
Take advantage of his distraction: anger never
Guarded itself well.

Let our wisest men
Know that tomorrow is the last of many battles
That we mean to fight: in our ranks there are,
Of those who until recently served Mark Antony,
Enough to bring him in. See it done:
And give the army a feast; we have the supplies to do it,
And they have earned the indulgence. Poor Antony!

SCENE II. Alexandria. CLEOPATRA's palace.

Enter MARK ANTONY, CLEOPATRA, DOMITIUS ENOBARBUS, CHARMIAN, IRAS, ALEXAS, with others

MARK ANTONY
He will not fight with me, Domitius.

He will not fight with me, Domitius.

DOMITIUS ENOBARBUS
No.

No.

MARK ANTONY
Why should he not?

Why won't he?

DOMITIUS ENOBARBUS
He thinks, being twenty times of better fortune,
He is twenty men to one.

He thinks, since his fortune is twenty times better,
He is twenty men to one.

MARK ANTONY
To-morrow, soldier,
By sea and land I'll fight: or I will live,
Or bathe my dying honour in the blood
Shall make it live again. Woo't thou fight well?

Tomorrow, soldier,
By sea and land I'll fight: or I will live,
Or bathe my dying honor in the blood
That will make it live again. Will you fight well?

DOMITIUS ENOBARBUS
I'll strike, and cry 'Take all.'

I will order them to take everything.

MARK ANTONY
Well said; come on.
Call forth my household servants: let's to-night
Be bounteous at our meal.

Well said; come on.
Tell my household servants to come: tonight let's
Have a generous meal.

Enter three or four Servitors

Give me thy hand,
Thou hast been rightly honest;--so hast thou;--

Thou,--and thou,--and thou:--you have served me well,

And kings have been your fellows.

Give me your hand,
You have been honest as you should be; --so have you;--
You,--and you, --and you:--you have served me well,
And you have been side-by-side with kings.

CLEOPATRA
[Aside to DOMITIUS ENOBARBUS]
What means this?

What is this about?

DOMITIUS ENOBARBUS
[Aside to CLEOPATRA]

'Tis one of those odd
tricks which sorrow shoots
Out of the mind.

MARK ANTONY
And thou art honest too.
I wish I could be made so many men,
And all of you clapp'd up together in
An Antony, that I might do you service
So good as you have done.

All
The gods forbid!

MARK ANTONY
Well, my good fellows, wait on me to-night:
Scant not my cups; and make as much of me
As when mine empire was your fellow too,
And suffer'd my command.

CLEOPATRA
[Aside to DOMITIUS ENOBARBUS]
What does he mean?

DOMITIUS ENOBARBUS
[Aside to CLEOPATRA]
To make his followers weep.

MARK ANTONY
Tend me to-night;
May be it is the period of your duty:
Haply you shall not see me more; or if,
A mangled shadow: perchance to-morrow
You'll serve another master. I look on you
As one that takes his leave. Mine honest friends,

I turn you not away; but, like a master
Married to your good service, stay till death:

Tend me to-night two hours, I ask no more,

And the gods yield you for't!

DOMITIUS ENOBARBUS
What mean you, sir,
To give them this discomfort? Look, they weep;
And I, an ass, am onion-eyed: for shame,
Transform us not to women.

MARK ANTONY

It is one of the odd
tricks that sadness shoots
Out of the mind.

And you are honest, too.
I wish I could be made into many men,
And all of you put together into
One Antony, so that I could serve you
As well as you have done.

May the gods forbid!

Well, my good men, wait on my tonight:
Keep my cups filled; and make as big a deal of me
As when my empire was yours too,
And was under my command.

What does he mean?

To make his followers cry.

Take care of me tonight;
It might be the last part of your service:
You may not see me again; or if you do,
Just a beaten shadow: perhaps tomorrow
You'll serve another master. I look at you
In the way of someone who is saying goodbye. My
honest friends,
I do not push you away; but, like a master
Depending on your good service, stay till my
death:
Care for me tonight for two hours, I do not ask for
more,
And may the gods treat you well for it!

What is the meaning of this, sir,
To make them so uncomfortable? Look, they cry;
And I myself am teary-eyed: for shame,
Don't make us like women.

Ho, ho, ho!
Now the witch take me, if I meant it thus!
Grace grow where those drops fall!
My hearty friends,
You take me in too dolorous a sense;
For I spake to you for your comfort; did desire you
To burn this night with torches: know, my hearts,
I hope well of to-morrow; and will lead you
Where rather I'll expect victorious life
Than death and honour. Let's to supper, come,

And drown consideration.

Exeunt

Hey, hey, hey!
Now the witch take me, if I meant it like that!
May good things grow where those drops fall!
My strong friends,
You misunderstand me in too sad a way;
For I spoke to you for your comfort; I wanted you
To fill this night with torches; know, my hearts,
I have good hopes of tomorrow; and will lead you
Where I expect a victorious life
Rather than an honorable death. Let's go to supper, come,
And drink away our worries.

SCENE III. The same. Before the palace.

Enter two Soldiers to their guard

First Soldier
Brother, good night: to-morrow is the day.

Brother, goodnight: tomorrow is the day.

Second Soldier
It will determine one way: fare you well.
Heard you of nothing strange about the streets?

One way or another, yes: farewell.
Have you not heard anything strange around the streets?

First Soldier
Nothing. What news?

Nothing. What news?

Second Soldier
Belike 'tis but a rumour. Good night to you.

Probably just a rumor. Goodnight.

First Soldier
Well, sir, good night.

Enter two other Soldiers

Second Soldier
Soldiers, have careful watch.

Soldiers, guard carefully.

Third Soldier
And you. Good night, good night.

They place themselves in every corner of the stage

Fourth Soldier
Here we: and if to-morrow
Our navy thrive, I have an absolute hope
Our landmen will stand up.

Here we are: and if tomorrow
Our navy does well, I have a firm hope
That our infantry will stand up.

Third Soldier
'Tis a brave army,
And full of purpose.

It is a brave army,
With strong conviction.

Music of the hautboys as under the stage

Fourth Soldier
Peace! what noise?

Quiet! What noise?

First Soldier
List, list!

Be still, be still!

Second Soldier
Hark!

Listen!

First Soldier

Music i' the air.

Third Soldier
Under the earth.

Fourth Soldier
It signs well, does it not?

Third Soldier
No.

First Soldier
Peace, I say!
What should this mean?

Second Soldier
'Tis the god Hercules, whom Antony loved,
Now leaves him.

First Soldier
Walk; let's see if other watchmen
Do hear what we do?

Second Soldier
How now, masters!

All
[Speaking together]
How now!
How now! do you hear this?

First Soldier
Ay; is't not strange?

Third Soldier
Do you hear, masters? do you hear?

First Soldier
Follow the noise so far as we have quarter;
Let's see how it will give off.

All
Content. 'Tis strange.

Exeunt

Music in the air.

Underground.

It's a good sign, right?

No.

Enough, I say!
What does this mean?

It's the god Hercules, whom Antony loved,
Now leaving him.

Walk; let's see if other guards
They advance to another post

What's going on, men?

What?
What? Do you hear this?

Yes, isn't it strange?

Do you hear, men? Do you hear?

Follow the noise as far as we are able;
Let's see how it will go off.

Stopped. It's strange.

SCENE IV. The same. A room in the palace.

Enter MARK ANTONY and CLEOPATRA, CHARMIAN, and others attending

MARK ANTONY
Eros! mine armour, Eros!

Eros! Get my armor, Eros!

CLEOPATRA
Sleep a little.

Sleep a little.

MARK ANTONY
No, my chuck. Eros, come; mine armour, Eros!

No, my darling. Eros, come; my armor, Eros!

Enter EROS with armour

Come good fellow, put mine iron on:
If fortune be not ours to-day, it is
Because we brave her: come.

Come, my good man, put my armor on:
If fortune is not ours today, it is
Because we challenger her: come.

CLEOPATRA
Nay, I'll help too.
What's this for?

No, I'll help too.
What's this for?

MARK ANTONY
Ah, let be, let be! thou art
The armourer of my heart: false, false; this, this.

Ah, leave it, leave it! You are
The armorer of my heart: wrong, wrong; this, this.

CLEOPATRA
Sooth, la, I'll help: thus it must be.

All right, now, I'll help: this is how it must be.

MARK ANTONY
Well, well;
We shall thrive now. Seest thou, my good fellow?
Go put on thy defences.

Well, well;
We will succeed now. Do you see, my good man?
Go put on your defenses.

EROS
Briefly, sir.

Quickly, sir.

CLEOPATRA
Is not this buckled well?

Isn't this buckled well?

MARK ANTONY
Rarely, rarely:
He that unbuckles this, till we do please
To daff't for our repose, shall hear a storm.
Thou fumblest, Eros; and my queen's a squire
More tight at this than thou: dispatch. O love,

Unusually well:
He that unbuckles this, until we choose
To take if off for rest, will hear a storm.
You fumble, Eros; and my queen's a squire
Who can do this better than you: go on. Oh, love,

That thou couldst see my wars to-day, and knew'st
The royal occupation! thou shouldst see
A workman in't.

Enter an armed Soldier

Good morrow to thee; welcome:
Thou look'st like him that knows a warlike charge:
To business that we love we rise betime,
And go to't with delight.

Soldier
A thousand, sir,
Early though't be, have on their riveted trim,
And at the port expect you.

Shout. Trumpets flourish
Enter Captains and Soldiers

Captain
The morn is fair. Good morrow, general.

All
Good morrow, general.

MARK ANTONY
'Tis well blown, lads:
This morning, like the spirit of a youth
That means to be of note, begins betimes.
So, so; come, give me that: this way; well said.
Fare thee well, dame, whate'er becomes of me:
This is a soldier's kiss: rebukeable

Kisses her

And worthy shameful cheque it were, to stand
On more mechanic compliment; I'll leave thee
Now, like a man of steel. You that will fight,
Follow me close; I'll bring you to't. Adieu.

Exeunt MARK ANTONY, EROS, Captains, and Soldiers

CHARMIAN
Please you, retire to your chamber.

CLEOPATRA
Lead me.
He goes forth gallantly. That he and Caesar might
Determine this great war in single fight!
Then Antony,--but now--Well, on.

If only you could see my wars today, and knew
The royal occupoation! You would see
A workman in it.

Good morning to you; welcome;
You look like a man who knows the ways of war:
We get up early to do things we love,
And go to it with delight.

A thousand men, sir,
Even though it is early, have their armor on,
And expect you at the port.

Beautiful weather. Good morning, general.

Good morning, general.

It is well bloomed, boys:
This morning, like the spirit of a young man
That means to make a good name for himself.
So, so; come, give me that: this way; well said.
Farewell, lady, whatever happens to me;
This is a solider's kiss: a bad

Think it would be, to stand
On a more meaningless compliment; I'll leave you
Now, like a man of steel. You who will fight,
Follow me closely; I'll bring you to it. Farewell.

Please, go rest in your room.

Lead me.
He goes out bravely. If only he and Caesar might
Determine this great war in a single battle!
Then Antony, -- but now -- Well, so it goes.

Exeunt

SCENE V. Alexandria. MARK ANTONY's camp.

Trumpets sound. Enter MARK ANTONY and EROS; a Soldier meeting them

Soldier
The gods make this a happy day to Antony!

May the gods make this a happy day to Antony!

MARK ANTONY
Would thou and those thy scars had once prevail'd
To make me fight at land!

*If only you and your scars had convinced me
To fight at land!*

Soldier
Hadst thou done so,
The kings that have revolted, and the soldier
That has this morning left thee, would have still
Follow'd thy heels.

*If you had done that,
The kings that have rebelled, and the soldier
That left you this morning would still have
Followed after you.*

MARK ANTONY
Who's gone this morning?

Who left this morning?

Soldier
Who!
One ever near thee: call for Enobarbus,

He shall not hear thee; or from Caesar's camp
Say 'I am none of thine.'

*Who!
One who was always near you: call for
Enobarbus,
He will not hear you; or from Caesar's camp
Say 'I am not one of yours.'*

MARK ANTONY
What say'st thou?

What do you say?

Soldier
Sir,
He is with Caesar.

*Sir,
He is with Caesar.*

EROS
Sir, his chests and treasure
He has not with him.

*Sir, his chests and treasure
He has not taken it with him.*

MARK ANTONY
Is he gone?

Has he left?

Soldier
Most certain.

Certainly.

MARK ANTONY
Go, Eros, send his treasure after; do it;
Detain no jot, I charge thee: write to him--

*Go, Eros, send his treasure to him; do it;
Do not be delayed, please: write to him --*

I will subscribe--gentle adieus and greetings;
Say that I wish he never find more cause
To change a master. O, my fortunes have
Corrupted honest men! Dispatch.--Enobarbus!

Exeunt

I will dictate -- gentle goodbyes and greetings;
Say that I wish he never finds reason again
To find a new master. Oh, my fortunes have
Corrupted honest men! Send it off to Enobarbus!

SCENE VI. Alexandria. OCTAVIUS CAESAR's camp.

Flourish. Enter OCTAVIUS CAESAR, AGRIPPA, with DOMITIUS ENOBARBUS, and others

OCTAVIUS CAESAR
Go forth, Agrippa, and begin the fight:
Our will is Antony be took alive;
Make it so known.

Go forward, Agrippa, and begin the fight:
We want Antony to be taken alive;
Make that known to all.

AGRIPPA
Caesar, I shall.

Caesar, I will.

Exit

OCTAVIUS CAESAR
The time of universal peace is near:
Prove this a prosperous day, the three-nook'd world

Shall bear the olive freely.

The time of worldwide peace is near:
If this is a successful day, the three-cornered
world
Will carry the olive branch freely.

Enter a Messenger

Messenger
Antony
Is come into the field.

Antony
Has come into the battle.

OCTAVIUS CAESAR
Go charge Agrippa
Plant those that have revolted in the van,

That Antony may seem to spend his fury
Upon himself.

Go tell Agrippa
Put those who have rebelled against him in the
front
So that Antony may seem to be fighting
Against himself.

Exeunt all but DOMITIUS ENOBARBUS

DOMITIUS ENOBARBUS
Alexas did revolt; and went to Jewry on
Affairs of Antony; there did persuade
Great Herod to incline himself to Caesar,
And leave his master Antony: for this pains
Caesar hath hang'd him. Canidius and the rest
That fell away have entertainment, but
No honourable trust. I have done ill;
Of which I do accuse myself so sorely,
That I will joy no more.

Alexas did rebel; and went to the Jewish lands on
Antony's business; and there persuaded
Great Herod to follow Caesar,
And leave his master Antony: for this effort
Caesar has hanged him. Canidius and the rest
That left now have work, but
No honorable trust. I have done poorly;
Of which I so terribly accuse myself,
I will never be happy again.

Enter a Soldier of CAESAR's

Soldier
Enobarbus, Antony
Hath after thee sent all thy treasure, with
His bounty overplus: the messenger
Came on my guard; and at thy tent is now
Unloading of his mules.

DOMITIUS ENOBARBUS
I give it you.

Soldier
Mock not, Enobarbus.
I tell you true: best you safed the bringer

Out of the host; I must attend mine office,
Or would have done't myself. Your emperor
Continues still a Jove.

Exit

DOMITIUS ENOBARBUS
I am alone the villain of the earth,
And feel I am so most. O Antony,
Thou mine of bounty, how wouldst thou have paid
My better service, when my turpitude
Thou dost so crown with gold! This blows my heart:

If swift thought break it not, a swifter mean
Shall outstrike thought: but thought will do't, I feel.
I fight against thee! No: I will go seek
Some ditch wherein to die; the foul'st best fits
My latter part of life.

Exit

Enobarbus, Mark Antony
Has send all your treasure to you, with
Extra from his own fortune: the messenger
Came during my guard; and at your tent is now
Unloading his mules.

I give it you.

Do not make fun of me, Enobarbus.
I tell you truly: it would be best if you helped the bringer
Leave here safely; I must go do my duties,
Or would have done it myself. Your emperor
Continues to be a god.

I am the worst villain on earth,
And feel terrible. Oh, Antony,
You gave me my riches, how you would have paid
My better service, when my betrayal
You crown with gold like this! This destroys my heart;
If quick thought doesn't break it, a quicker action
Will outdo thought: but thought will do it, I feel.
I fight against you! No: I will go look for
Some ditch where I can die; the dirt best fits
The end of my life.

SCENE VII. Field of battle between the camps.

Alarum. Drums and trumpets. Enter AGRIPPA and others

AGRIPPA
Retire, we have engaged ourselves too far:
Caesar himself has work, and our oppression
Exceeds what we expected.

Fall back, we have spread ourselves too far:
Caesar himself has work, and our opposition
Is more than what we expected.

Exeunt
Alarums. Enter MARK ANTONY and SCARUS wounded

SCARUS
O my brave emperor, this is fought indeed!
Had we done so at first, we had droven them home

With clouts about their heads.

Oh, my brave emperor, this is fighting indeed!
If we had done so from the first, we would have
driven them home
With bruises around their heads.

MARK ANTONY
Thou bleed'st apace.

You're bleeding.

SCARUS
I had a wound here that was like a T,
But now 'tis made an H.

I had a wound here that was like a T,
But now it is an H.

MARK ANTONY
They do retire.

Then go rest.

SCARUS
We'll beat 'em into bench-holes: I have yet
Room for six scotches more.

We'll beat them back: I still have
Room for six more scratches.

Enter EROS

EROS
They are beaten, sir, and our advantage serves
For a fair victory.

They are beaten, sir, and our advantage serves
For a glorious victory.

SCARUS
Let us score their backs,
And snatch 'em up, as we take hares, behind:

'Tis sport to maul a runner.

Let us wound their backs,
And snatch them up, the way we catch rabbits,
from behind:
It's fun to maul a runner

MARK ANTONY

I will reward thee
Once for thy spritely comfort, and ten-fold

For thy good valour. Come thee on.

SCARUS
I'll halt after.

Exeunt

I will reward you
Once for your cheerful comfort, and ten times
more
For your bravery. Come one.

I'll follow after.

SCENE VIII. Under the walls of Alexandria.

Alarum. Enter MARK ANTONY, in a march; SCARUS, with others

MARK ANTONY
We have beat him to his camp: run one before,
And let the queen know of our guests. To-morrow,

Before the sun shall see 's, we'll spill the blood
That has to-day escaped. I thank you all;
For doughty-handed are you, and have fought
Not as you served the cause, but as 't had been

Each man's like mine; you have shown all Hectors.

Enter the city, clip your wives, your friends,
Tell them your feats; whilst they with joyful tears
Wash the congealment from your wounds, and kiss
The honour'd gashes whole.

To SCARUS

Give me thy hand

Enter CLEOPATRA, attended

To this great fairy I'll commend thy acts,
Make her thanks bless thee.

To CLEOPATRA

O thou day o' the world,
Chain mine arm'd neck; leap thou, attire and all,
Through proof of harness to my heart, and there
Ride on the pants triumphing!

CLEOPATRA
Lord of lords!
O infinite virtue, comest thou smiling from
The world's great snare uncaught?

MARK ANTONY
My nightingale,
We have beat them to their beds.
What, girl! though grey

We have beaten him to his camp: run ahead,
And let the queen know about our guests.
Tomorrow
Before the sun shall see it, we'll spill the blood
That has escaped today. I thank you all;
For you are brave and tough, and have fought
Not as if you were serving the cause, but as if it
had been
Your own the way it is mine; you have shown
yourselves as great warriors.
Enter the city, go see your wives, your friends,
Tell them you deeds; while they with joyful tears
Wash the scabs from your wounds, and kiss
The honored cuts whole.

Give me your hand

To this woman I'll praise your actions,
May her thanks bless you.

Oh you day of the world,
Put an arm around my neck; jump, clothes and all
Through the armor to my heart, and there
Ride on my chariot in victory!

Lord of lords!
Oh wonderful, do you come smiling from
The world's big trap without being caught?

My nightingale,
We have beaten them to their beds.
What, girl! Even if gray

Do something mingle with our younger brown,
yet ha' we
A brain that nourishes our nerves, and can
Get goal for goal of youth. Behold this man;
Commend unto his lips thy favouring hand:
Kiss it, my warrior: he hath fought to-day
As if a god, in hate of mankind, had
Destroy'd in such a shape.

CLEOPATRA
I'll give thee, friend,
An armour all of gold; it was a king's.

MARK ANTONY
He has deserved it, were it carbuncled
Like holy Phoebus' car. Give me thy hand:
Through Alexandria make a jolly march;
Bear our hack'd targets like the men that owe them:

Had our great palace the capacity
To camp this host, we all would sup together,
And drink carouses to the next day's fate,
Which promises royal peril. Trumpeters,
With brazen din blast you the city's ear;
Make mingle with rattling tabourines;
That heaven and earth may strike their sounds together,

Applauding our approach.

Exeunt

Some of our hair mixes with younger-looking
brown, yet we have
A brain that feeds our nerves, and can
Match against youth. Look at this man;
Allow him to touch your hand with his lips:
Kiss it, my warrior: he has fought today
As if a god, hating mankind, had
Destroyed it in the shape of a man.

I'll give you, friend,
A set of armor made out of gold; it was a king's.

He deserves it, even if it were covered in jewels
Like holy Phoebus' chariot. Give me your hand:
Let us cheerfully march through Alexandria;
Carry our damaged targets like the men what owe
them:
If our huge palace had the room
To host all these men, we would all eat together,
And drink in celebration of the next day's fate,
Which promises royal danger. Trumpeters,
With loudness blast the city's ear;
Mix the sounds with rattling tambourines;
That heaven and earth may hit their sounds
together,
Applauding our approach.

SCENE IX. OCTAVIUS CAESAR's camp.

Sentinels at their post

First Soldier
If we be not relieved within this hour,
We must return to the court of guard: the night
Is shiny; and they say we shall embattle
By the second hour i' the morn.

If we are not replaced within the hour,
We must return to our tent: the night
Is bright; and they say we will go into battle
By the second hour of the morning.

Second Soldier
This last day was
A shrewd one to's.

This last day was
A difficult one too.

Enter DOMITIUS ENOBARBUS

DOMITIUS ENOBARBUS
O, bear me witness, night,--

Oh, witness me, night,--

Third Soldier
What man is this?

Who is this?

Second Soldier
Stand close, and list him.

Stand close, and listen to him.

DOMITIUS ENOBARBUS
Be witness to me, O thou blessed moon,
When men revolted shall upon record
Bear hateful memory, poor Enobarbus did
Before thy face repent!

Be witness to me, oh you blessed moon,
When men who rebelled shall in history
Be remembered with hate, poor Enobarbus did
Repent in front of you!

First Soldier
Enobarbus!

Enobarbus!

Third Soldier
Peace!
Hark further.

Quiet!
Keep listening.

DOMITIUS ENOBARBUS
O sovereign mistress of true melancholy,
The poisonous damp of night disponge upon me,
That life, a very rebel to my will,
May hang no longer on me: throw my heart
Against the flint and hardness of my fault:

Oh ruling mistress of true gloominess,
May that poisonous damp of night take from me,
So that life, a rebel against my will,
May not stay with me any longer: throw my heart
Against the stone hardness of my fault:

Which, being dried with grief, will break to powder,

And finish all foul thoughts. O Antony,
Nobler than my revolt is infamous,
Forgive me in thine own particular;
But let the world rank me in register
A master-leaver and a fugitive:
O Antony! O Antony!

Dies

Second Soldier
Let's speak to him.

First Soldier
Let's hear him, for the things he speaks
May concern Caesar.

Third Soldier
Let's do so. But he sleeps.

First Soldier
Swoons rather; for so bad a prayer as his
Was never yet for sleep.

Second Soldier
Go we to him.

Third Soldier
Awake, sir, awake; speak to us.

Second Soldier
Hear you, sir?

First Soldier
The hand of death hath raught him.

Drums afar off

Hark! the drums
Demurely wake the sleepers. Let us bear him
To the court of guard; he is of note: our hour
Is fully out.

Third Soldier
Come on, then;
He may recover yet.

Exeunt with the body

Which, being dried with grief, will break to powder,
And finish all bad thoughts. Oh Antony,
More noble than my rebellion is terrible,
Forgive me as you wish;
But let the world consider me
A deserter and traitor:
O Antony! O Antony!

Let's talk to him.

Let's listen to him, for the things he speaks
Might have to do with Caesar.

We should. But he sleeps.

Faints, I think; for a prayer as dark as his
Was not meant for sleep.

We should go to him.

Wake up, sir, wake up; speak to us.

Do you hear, sir?

He's dead.

Listen! The drums
Politely wake the sleepers. Let us carry him
To the guard's tent; he is important; our our
Is now ended.

Come on, then;
He might still recover.

SCENE X. Between the two camps.

Enter MARK ANTONY and SCARUS, with their Army

MARK ANTONY
Their preparation is to-day by sea;
We please them not by land.

They plan today to fight by sea;
They do not like fighting us by land.

SCARUS
For both, my lord.

For both, sir.

MARK ANTONY
I would they'ld fight i' the fire or i' the air;
We'ld fight there too. But this it is; our foot

Upon the hills adjoining to the city
Shall stay with us: order for sea is given;
They have put forth the haven
Where their appointment we may best discover,
And look on their endeavour.

I wish they would fight us in the fire or in the air;
We would fight there too. But this is how it is; our
infantry
On the hills beside the city
Will stay with us: I have ordered for sea;
They have put forward the safe place
Where we might best find them,
And look at their efforts.

Exeunt

SCENE XI. Another part of the same.

Enter OCTAVIUS CAESAR, and his Army

OCTAVIUS CAESAR
But being charged, we will be still by land,
Which, as I take't, we shall; for his best force
Is forth to man his galleys. To the vales,
And hold our best advantage.

Exeunt

But by being charged, we should still fight by land,
Which, as I take it, we will; for his best force
Has gone to staff his ships. To the valleys,
And hold our best advantage.

SCENE XII. Another part of the same.

Enter MARK ANTONY and SCARUS

MARK ANTONY
Yet they are not join'd: where yond pine does stand,

I shall discover all: I'll bring thee word

Straight, how 'tis like to go.

Exit

SCARUS
Swallows have built
In Cleopatra's sails their nests: the augurers
Say they know not, they cannot tell; look grimly,

And dare not speak their knowledge. Antony
Is valiant, and dejected; and, by starts,
His fretted fortunes give him hope, and fear,
Of what he has, and has not.

Re-enter MARK ANTONY

MARK ANTONY
All is lost;
This foul Egyptian hath betrayed me:
My fleet hath yielded to the foe; and yonder
They cast their caps up and carouse together
Like friends long lost. Triple-turn'd whore!
'tis thou
Hast sold me to this novice; and my heart
Makes only wars on thee. Bid them all fly;

For when I am revenged upon my charm,
I have done all. Bid them all fly; begone.

Exit SCARUS

O sun, thy uprise shall I see no more:
Fortune and Antony part here; even here
Do we shake hands. All come to this? The hearts

That spaniel'd me at heels, to whom I gave

Yet they have not shown up: where the pine tree over there stands,
I will find out what's going on: I will bring you news
Immediately, how things are likely to be.

Swallows have built
Their nests in Cleopatra's sails: the fortune-tellers
Say they have no idea what this means; they look grim
And do not dare say what they know. Antony
Is courageous, and worried; and, alternating,
His seesawing luck gives him hope, and fear,
Alarum afar off, as at a sea-fight

All is lost;
This terrible Egyptian has betrayed me:
My fleet has given up to the enemy; and over there
They throw their hats up and celebrate together
Like long-lost friends. Three times a whore!
It is you
That have sold me to this newcomer, and my heart
Does nothing but fight against you. Tell them all to run;
For when I have revenge on that witch,
I will have done all. Tell them all to run; go.

Oh sun, I will not see you rise ever again;
Destiny and Antony separate here: here
We shake hands. Has it all come to this? The hearts
That loyally followed me, to whom I have

Their wishes, do discandy, melt their sweets
On blossoming Caesar; and this pine is bark'd,
That overtopp'd them all. Betray'd I am:
O this false soul of Egypt! this grave charm,--

Whose eye beck'd forth my wars, and call'd them
home;
Whose bosom was my crownet, my chief end,--
Like a right gipsy, hath, at fast and loose,
Beguiled me to the very heart of loss.
What, Eros, Eros!

Enter CLEOPATRA

Ah, thou spell! Avaunt!

CLEOPATRA
Why is my lord enraged against his love?

MARK ANTONY
Vanish, or I shall give thee thy deserving,
And blemish Caesar's triumph. Let him take thee,

And hoist thee up to the shouting plebeians:

Follow his chariot, like the greatest spot
Of all thy sex; most monster-like, be shown
For poor'st diminutives, for doits; and let
Patient Octavia plough thy visage up
With her prepared nails.

Exit CLEOPATRA

'Tis well thou'rt gone,
If it be well to live; but better 'twere
Thou fell'st into my fury, for one death
Might have prevented many. Eros, ho!
The shirt of Nessus is upon me: teach me,
Alcides, thou mine ancestor, thy rage:
Let me lodge Lichas on the horns o' the moon;
And with those hands, that grasp'd the heaviest club,
Subdue my worthiest self. The witch shall die:
To the young Roman boy she hath sold me, and I fall
Under this plot; she dies for't. Eros, ho!

Exit

Everything they wanted, now turn and serve
Blooming Caesar; and this pine has bark,
That towered over them all. I am betrayed:
Oh this lying soul of Egypt! This bewitching spell,
--
Whose eyes brought my wars, and called them
home;
Whose bosom was my most important goal,--
Like a gypsy, has, fast and loose,
Tricked me to the very deepest loss.
What, Eros, Eros!

You witch! Go!

Why is my lord angry with his love?

Go, or I will give you what you deserve,
And put a stain on Caesar's triumph. Let him take
you,
And stick you up on a pole in front of the shouting
commoners:
Follow his chariot, like the worst example
Of all womanhood; like a monster, be shown
To frighten the smallest; and let
Patient Octavia claw your face off
With her manicured nails.

It is good that you are gone,
If it is good to live; but it would be better
If you fell into my fury, for one death
Might have prevented many. Eros, hey!
The armor of Nessus is on me: teach me,
Alcides, my ancestor, your rage:
Let me stick Lichas on the horns of the moon;
And with those hands, that held the heaviest club,
Push down my better self. The witch must die:
She has sold me to the young roman boy, and I fall
Because of this plot; she must die for it. Eros, hey!

SCENE XIII. Alexandria. Cleopatra's palace.

Enter CLEOPATRA, CHARMIAN, IRAS, and MARDIAN

CLEOPATRA
Help me, my women! O, he is more mad
Than Telamon for his shield; the boar of Thessaly
Was never so emboss'd.

CHARMIAN
To the monument!
There lock yourself, and send him word you are dead.

The soul and body rive not more in parting
Than greatness going off.

CLEOPATRA
To the monument!
Mardian, go tell him I have slain myself;
Say, that the last I spoke was 'Antony,'
And word it, prithee, piteously: hence, Mardian,
And bring me how he takes my death.

To the monument!

Exeunt

Help me, my women! Oh, he is more insane
Than Telamon for his shield; the boar of Thessaly
Was never carved like that.

To the monument!
Lock yourself in there, and send him a message
that you are dead.
The soul and body do not rival more in separating
Than greatness ending.

To the monument!
Mardian, go tell him I have killed myself:
Say that the last thing I said was 'Antony,'
And please, make it sound very sad: go, Mardian,
And bring back the news of how he takes my
death.
To the monument!

SCENE XIV. The same. Another room.

Enter MARK ANTONY and EROS

MARK ANTONY
Eros, thou yet behold'st me?

Eros, you would still look at me?

EROS
Ay, noble lord.

Yes, noble lord.

MARK ANTONY
Sometimes we see a cloud that's dragonish;

A vapour sometime like a bear or lion,
A tower'd citadel, a pendent rock,
A forked mountain, or blue promontory
With trees upon't, that nod unto the world,
And mock our eyes with air: thou hast seen these signs;

They are black vesper's pageants.

Sometimes we see a cloud that looks like a dragon;
A mist sometimes like a bear or lion,
A city with towers, a tall rock,
A forked mountain, or blue cliff
With trees on it, that nod to the world,
And tease our eyes with air: you have seen things like this;
They are the theater of nature.

EROS
Ay, my lord,

Yes, my lord.

MARK ANTONY
My good knave Eros, now thy captain is
Even such a body: here I am Antony:
Yet cannot hold this visible shape, my knave.
I made these wars for Egypt: and the queen,--
Whose heart I thought I had, for she had mine;
Which whilst it was mine had annex'd unto't
A million more, now lost,--she, Eros, has
Pack'd cards with Caesar, and false-play'd my glory
Unto an enemy's triumph.
Nay, weep not, gentle Eros; there is left us
Ourselves to end ourselves.

My good servant Eros, now your captain is
A body like that: here I am Antony:
Yet cannot hold this shape you see, my servant.
I made these wars for Egypt: and the queen,--
Whose heart I thought I had, for she had mine;
Which while it was mine had shared with it
A million more, now lost,--she, Eros, has
Joined in with Caesar, and tricked my glory
Into an enemy's victory.
No, do not cry, gentle Eros; we still have
The ability to end ourselves.

Enter MARDIAN

O! thy vile lady!
She has robb'd me of my sword.

Oh, your terrible lady!
She has robbed my sword from me.

MARDIAN
No, Antony;
My mistress loved thee, and her fortunes mingled
With thine entirely.

No, Mark Antony;
My lady loved you, and combined her destiny
With yours completely.

MARK ANTONY
Hence, saucy eunuch; peace!
She hath betray'd me and shall die the death.

MARDIAN
Death of one person can be paid but once,
And that she has discharged: what thou wouldst do
Is done unto thy hand: the last she spake
Was 'Antony! most noble Antony!'
Then in the midst a tearing groan did break
The name of Antony; it was divided
Between her heart and lips: she render'd life,
Thy name so buried in her.

MARK ANTONY
Dead, then?

MARDIAN
Dead.

MARK ANTONY
Unarm, Eros; the long day's task is done,

And we must sleep.

To MARDIAN

That thou depart'st hence safe,
Does pay thy labour richly; go.

Exit MARDIAN

Off, pluck off:
The seven-fold shield of Ajax cannot keep
The battery from my heart. O, cleave, my sides!
Heart, once be stronger than thy continent,
Crack thy frail case! Apace, Eros, apace.
No more a soldier: bruised pieces, go;
You have been nobly borne. From me awhile.

Exit EROS

I will o'ertake thee, Cleopatra, and
Weep for my pardon. So it must be, for now

All length is torture: since the torch is out,
Lie down, and stray no farther: now all labour
Mars what it does; yea, very force entangles
Itself with strength: seal then, and all is done.

Go, saucy eunuch; quiet!
She has betrayed me and must die.

One person can only die once,
And that she has done: what you would do
Has been done for you: the last thing she said
Was 'Antony! Most noble Antony!'
Then in the middle of a last groan broke
The name of Antony; it was split
Between her heart and her lips: she gave up life
With your name buried like that in her.

Dead, ten?

Dead.

Take off my armor, Eros; the long day's task is done
And we must sleep.

That you leave here safely,
Repays you well; go.

Off, take it off:
The thickest shield of Ajax cannot keep
The wound from my heart. Oh, split, my sides!
Heart, once stronger than you needed to be,
Crack your weak case! Away, Eros, away.
I am no longer a soldier, just bruised pieces, go;
You have done well. Go away from me awhile.

I will catch up to you, Cleopatra, and
Cry for forgiveness. This is how it must me, for now
Just existing is torture: since the torch is out,
Lie down, and go no farther away: now all work
Ruins what it does; yes, force tangles
Itself with strength: stop everything then, and all is done.

Eros!--I come, my queen:--Eros!--Stay for me:

Where souls do couch on flowers, we'll hand in hand,

And with our sprightly port make the ghosts gaze:

And all the haunt be ours. Come, Eros, Eros!

Re-enter EROS

EROS
What would my lord?

MARK ANTONY
Since Cleopatra died,
I have lived in such dishonour, that the gods
Detest my baseness. I, that with my sword

Quarter'd the world, and o'er green Neptune's back

With ships made cities, condemn myself to lack

The courage of a woman; less noble mind

Than she which by her death our Caesar tells
'I am conqueror of myself.' Thou art sworn, Eros,

That, when the exigent should come, which now
Is come indeed, when I should see behind me
The inevitable prosecution of
Disgrace and horror, that, on my command,
Thou then wouldst kill me: do't; the time is come:
Thou strikest not me, 'tis Caesar thou defeat'st.

Put colour in thy cheek.

EROS
The gods withhold me!
Shall I do that which all the Parthian darts,
Though enemy, lost aim, and could not?

MARK ANTONY
Eros,
Wouldst thou be window'd in great Rome and see
Thy master thus with pleach'd arms, bending down
His corrigible neck, his face subdued
To penetrative shame, whilst the wheel'd seat
Of fortunate Caesar, drawn before him, branded
His baseness that ensued?

Eros! -- I'm coming, my queen: -- Eros! Stay for me:
Where souls rest on flowers, we'll go hand in hand,
And with our energetic walk make the ghosts stare:
And all the haunting will be ours. Come, Eros, Eros!

What does my lord wish?

Since Cleopata died,
I have lived in such dishonor that all the gods
Are disgusted by my lowliness. I, who with my sword
Divided the world into four pieces, and over the green sea
Made cities with ships, condemn myself for lacking
The courage of a woman; having a less noble mind
Than she who by her death our Caesar tells
'I have conquered myself.' You have promised, Eros,
That, when the desperate time came, which now
Has come indeed, when I see behind me
The impossible-to-stop time of
Disgrace and horror, that, if I ordered you,
You would then kill me: do it; the time has come:
You're not attacking me, it's Caesar you're defeating.
Put color in your cheek.

May the gods prevent me!
Must I do what all the Parthian arrows
Though enemy, lost aim, and could not?

Eros,
Do you want to be in great Rome and see
Your master like this with tied arms, bending down
His losing neck, his face brought
To complete shame, while the wheeled seat
Of lucky Caesar, pulled in front of him, burned
The defeat that came after?

EROS
I would not see't.

I do not want to see it.

MARK ANTONY
Come, then; for with a wound I must be cured.
Draw that thy honest sword, which thou hast worn
Most useful for thy country.

Come, then; I must be cured with a wound.
Draw your honest sword, which you have worn
Very usefully for your country.

EROS
O, sir, pardon me!

Oh, sir, forgive me!

MARK ANTONY
When I did make thee free, sworest thou not then
To do this when I bade thee? Do it at once;

Or thy precedent services are all
But accidents unpurposed. Draw, and come.

When I made you free, did you not swear then
To do this when I commanded you? Do it
immediately;
Or everything you have done before
No longer counts. Draw, and come.

EROS
Turn from me, then, that noble countenance,
Wherein the worship of the whole world lies.

Turn away from me, then, that noble face,
Where the worship of the whole world lies.

MARK ANTONY
Lo thee!

Look, you!

Turning from him

EROS
My sword is drawn.

My sword is drawn.

MARK ANTONY
Then let it do at once
The thing why thou hast drawn it.

Then let it do right now
The thing for which you have drawn it.

EROS
My dear master,
My captain, and my emperor, let me say,
Before I strike this bloody stroke, farewell.

My dear master,
My captain, and my emperor, let me say,
Before I strike this bloody stroke, goodbye.

MARK ANTONY
'Tis said, man; and farewell.

It is said, man; and farewell.

EROS
Farewell, great chief. Shall I strike now?

Farewell, great leader. Shall I strike now?

MARK ANTONY
Now, Eros.

Now, Eros.

EROS
Why, there then: thus I do escape the sorrow

Why, there then: in this way I escape the sadness

Of Antony's death.

Kills himself

MARK ANTONY
Thrice-nobler than myself!
Thou teachest me, O valiant Eros, what
I should, and thou couldst not. My queen and Eros
Have by their brave instruction got upon me
A nobleness in record: but I will be
A bridegroom in my death, and run into't
As to a lover's bed. Come, then; and, Eros,
Thy master dies thy scholar: to do thus

Three times nobler than myself!
You teach me, O brave Eros, what
I should do, and I could not. My queen and Eros
Have through their brave teaching got me
A history of nobleness: but I will be
A bridegroom in my death, and run into it
Like to a lover's bed. Come, then; and, Eros,
Your master dies you student: to do like this

Falling on his sword

I learn'd of thee. How! not dead? not dead?
The guard, ho! O, dispatch me!

That I learned of you. How! Not dead? Not dead?
Guards, hey! Oh, kill me!

Enter DERCETAS and Guard

First Guard
What's the noise?

What's that noise?

MARK ANTONY
I have done my work in, friends: O, make an end
Of what I have begun.

I have failed at my work, friends: oh, end
What I have begun.

Second Guard
The star is fall'n.

The star has fallen.

First Guard
And time is at his period.

And time has ended.

All
Alas, and woe!

Oh no!

MARK ANTONY
Let him that loves me strike me dead.

Let he that loves me strike me dead.

First Guard
Not I.

Not I.

Second Guard
Nor I.

Nor I.

Third Guard
Nor any one.

Nor anyone.

Exeunt Guard

DERCETAS

Thy death and fortunes bid thy followers fly.
This sword but shown to Caesar, with this tidings,
Shall enter me with him.

Enter DIOMEDES

DIOMEDES
Where's Antony?

Your death and destiny tells your followers to run,
This sword shown to Caesar, with this news,
Will make him favor me.

Where's Antony?

DERCETAS
There, Diomed there.

There, Diomed, there.

DIOMEDES
Lives he?
Wilt thou not answer, man?

Does he live?
Will you not answer, man?

Exit DERCETAS

MARK ANTONY
Art thou there, Diomed? Draw thy sword, and give me

Suffing strokes for death.

Are you there, Diomed? Pull out your sword, and
give me
Enough wounds to die.

DIOMEDES
Most absolute lord,
My mistress Cleopatra sent me to thee.

My leader,
My lady Cleopatra sent me to you.

MARK ANTONY
When did she send thee?

When did she send you?

DIOMEDES
Now, my lord.

Now, sir.

MARK ANTONY
Where is she?

Where is she?

DIOMEDES
Lock'd in her monument. She had a prophesying fear

Of what hath come to pass: for when she saw--
Which never shall be found--you did suspect
She had disposed with Caesar, and that your rage

Would not be purged, she sent you word she was dead;

But, fearing since how it might work, hath sent
Me to proclaim the truth; and I am come,
I dread, too late.

Locked in your monument. She had a predicting
fear
Of what has happened: because when she saw --
Which will never be found -- you suspected
She had negotiated with Caesar, and that your
rage
Would not be removed, she sent you a message
that she was dead;
But, afraid since then how it might work, has sent
Me to give the truth; and I have come,
I'm afraid, too late.

MARK ANTONY

Too late, good Diomed: call my guard, I prithee.

DIOMEDES
What, ho, the emperor's guard! The guard, what, ho!
Come, your lord calls!

Enter four or five of the Guard of MARK ANTONY

MARK ANTONY
Bear me, good friends, where Cleopatra bides;
'Tis the last service that I shall command you.

First Guard
Woe, woe are we, sir, you may not live to wear
All your true followers out.

All
Most heavy day!

MARK ANTONY
Nay, good my fellows, do not please sharp fate
To grace it with your sorrows: bid that welcome
Which comes to punish us, and we punish it
Seeming to bear it lightly. Take me up:
I have led you oft: carry me now, good friends,
And have my thanks for all.

Exeunt, bearing MARK ANTONY

Too late, good Diomed: call my guards, please.

Hey, the emperor's guards! The guards, hey!
Come, your lord calls!

Carry me, good friends, to where Cleopatra is;
It is the last thing I will tell you to do.

Sad, sad we are, sir, you may not live to exhaust
Your true followers.

Worst day!

No, my good men, do not please harsh fate
By rewarding it with your sadness: welcome what
Comes to punish us, and we punish it
By seeming to endure it easily. Pick me up:
I have led you often: carry me now, good friends,
And have my thanks for all.

SCENE XV. The same. A monument.

Enter CLEOPATRA and her maids aloft, with CHARMIAN and IRAS

CLEOPATRA
O Charmian, I will never go from hence.

Oh Charmian, I will never leave here.

CHARMIAN
Be comforted, dear madam.

Be comforted, dear lady.

CLEOPATRA
No, I will not:
All strange and terrible events are welcome,
But comforts we despise; our size of sorrow,
Proportion'd to our cause, must be as great
As that which makes it.

No, I won't:
All strange and terrible events are welcome,
But we despise comfort; our amount of sadness
The same size as our reason, must be as big
As the thing which makes it.

Enter, below, DIOMEDES

How now! is he dead?

What now? Is he dead?

DIOMEDES
His death's upon him, but not dead.
Look out o' the other side your monument;
His guard have brought him thither.

He is dying, but not dead.
Look out of the other side of your monument;
His guards have brought him there.

Enter, below, MARK ANTONY, borne by the Guard

CLEOPATRA
O sun,
Burn the great sphere thou movest in! darkling stand

The varying shore o' the world. O Antony,
Antony, Antony! Help, Charmian, help, Iras, help;
Help, friends below; let's draw him hither.

Oh sun,
Burn the part of the sky you move in! May darkly
stand
The wavering shore of the world. Oh, Antony,
Antony, Antony! Help, Charmian, help, Iras, help;
Help, friends below; let's bring him here.

MARK ANTONY
Peace!
Not Caesar's valour hath o'erthrown Antony,

But Antony's hath triumph'd on itself.

Quiet!
It is not Caesar's bravery that has overthrown
Antony,
But Antony's has won against itself.

CLEOPATRA
So it should be, that none but Antony

That is how it should be, that no one but Antony

Should conquer Antony; but woe 'tis so!

MARK ANTONY
I am dying, Egypt, dying; only
I here importune death awhile, until
Of many thousand kisses the poor last
I lay up thy lips.

CLEOPATRA
I dare not, dear,--
Dear my lord, pardon,--I dare not,
Lest I be taken: not the imperious show
Of the full-fortuned Caesar ever shall
Be brooch'd with me; if knife, drugs,
serpents, have
Edge, sting, or operation, I am safe:
Your wife Octavia, with her modest eyes
And still conclusion, shall acquire no honour
Demuring upon me. But come, come, Antony,--
Help me, my women,--we must draw thee up:
Assist, good friends.

MARK ANTONY
O, quick, or I am gone.

CLEOPATRA
Here's sport indeed! How heavy weighs my lord!
Our strength is all gone into heaviness,
That makes the weight: had I great Juno's power,

The strong-wing'd Mercury should fetch thee up,
And set thee by Jove's side. Yet come a little,--
Wishes were ever fools,--O, come, come, come;

They heave MARK ANTONY aloft to CLEOPATRA

And welcome, welcome! die where thou hast lived:

Quicken with kissing: had my lips that power,
Thus would I wear them out.

All
A heavy sight!

MARK ANTONY
I am dying, Egypt, dying:
Give me some wine, and let me speak a little.

CLEOPATRA
No, let me speak; and let me rail so high,

Would win over Antony; but how tragic for it to be that way!

I am dying, Egypt, dying; only
I here put off death for a while, until
Of many thousand kisses the last little one
I place on your lips.

I do not dare, dear, --
My dear, forgive me, -- I dare not
In case I am taken: not the ruling show
Of the victorious Caesar will ever
Use me; if knife, drugs,
snakes, have
Edge, sting, or operation, I am safe:
Your wife Octavia, with her humble and quiet eyes
And still behavior, shall not have any honor
Dishonoring me. But come, come, Antony, --
Help me, my women, -- we must pull you up:
Help, good friends.

Oh, be quick, or I will be gone.

Here is a game indeed! My lord is so heavy!
Our strength is all gone into that heaviness,
That makes the weight: if I had great Juno's power,
The strong-winged Mercury would pick you up
And put you by Jove's side. But come a little, --
Wishes were always fools, -- Oh, come, come, come;

And welcome, welcome! Die where you have lived:
Come alive with kissing: if my lips had that power,
This his how I would wear them out.

A tragic sight!

I am dying, Egypt, dying:
Give me some wine, and let me talk a little.

No, let me speak; and let me mourn so hard

That the false housewife Fortune break her wheel,
Provoked by my offence.

MARK ANTONY
One word, sweet queen:
Of Caesar seek your honour, with your safety. O!

CLEOPATRA
They do not go together.

MARK ANTONY
Gentle, hear me:
None about Caesar trust but Proculeius.

CLEOPATRA
My resolution and my hands I'll trust;
None about Caesar.

MARK ANTONY
The miserable change now at my end
Lament nor sorrow at; but please your thoughts
In feeding them with those my former fortunes

Wherein I lived, the greatest prince o' the world,
The noblest; and do now not basely die,
Not cowardly put off my helmet to
My countryman,--a Roman by a Roman

Valiantly vanquish'd. Now my spirit is going;
I can no more.

CLEOPATRA
Noblest of men, woo't die?
Hast thou no care of me? shall I abide

In this dull world, which in thy absence is
No better than a sty? O, see, my women,

MARK ANTONY dies

The crown o' the earth doth melt. My lord!
O, wither'd is the garland of the war,
The soldier's pole is fall'n: young boys and girls
Are level now with men; the odds is gone,
And there is nothing left remarkable
Beneath the visiting moon.

Faints

CHARMIAN

---

*That the false wife Fortune breaks her wheel,
Angered by my offense.*

*One word, sweet queen:
Go to Caesar and find your honor, with your
safety. Oh!*

They do not go together.

*Gentle one, listen to me:
Do not trust anyone around Caesar but
Proculeius.*

*I'll trust my resolve and my hands;
Not anyone around Caesar.*

*The miserable dying now at my end
Do not cry over; but please your thoughts
In feeding them with the ones of my former good
fortune
Where I lived, the greatest prince in the world,
The noblest; and do not now die without honor,
Not cowardly taken off my helmet to
Another man from my country -- A Roman by a
Roman
Bravely beaten. Now my spirit is going;
I can't any longer.*

*Most noble of men, would you die?
Do you have no care for me? Must I continue
living
In this dull world, which without you is
No better than a pigsty? Oh, see, my women,*

*The best man on Earth is gone. My lord!
Oh, withered is the garland of war,
The soldier's pole has fallen: young boys and girls
Are now equal with men; the odds are gone,
And there is nothing left good or special
Beneath the visiting moon.*

O, quietness, lady!

IRAS
She is dead too, our sovereign.

CHARMIAN
Lady!

IRAS
Madam!

CHARMIAN
O madam, madam, madam!

IRAS
Royal Egypt, Empress!

CHARMIAN
Peace, peace, Iras!

CLEOPATRA
No more, but e'en a woman, and commanded
By such poor passion as the maid that milks
And does the meanest chares. It were for me
To throw my sceptre at the injurious gods;
To tell them that this world did equal theirs
Till they had stol'n our jewel. All's but naught;

Patience is scottish, and impatience does
Become a dog that's mad: then is it sin
To rush into the secret house of death,
Ere death dare come to us? How do you, women?

What, what! good cheer! Why, how now, Charmian!

My noble girls! Ah, women, women, look,
Our lamp is spent, it's out! Good sirs, take heart:

We'll bury him; and then, what's brave, what's noble,

Let's do it after the high Roman fashion,
And make death proud to take us. Come, away:
This case of that huge spirit now is cold:

Ah, women, women! come; we have no friend
But resolution, and the briefest end.

Exeunt; those above bearing off MARK ANTONY's body

O, quietness, lady!

She is dead too, our royal leader.

Lady!

Madam!

Oh madam, madam, madam!

Royal Egypt, Empress!

Quiet, quiet, Iras!

No more, just a woman, and commanded
By such poor passion as a milkmaid
And the lowliest of servants. It was my fate
To throw my scepter at the wounding gods:
To tell them that this world equalled theirs
Till they had stolen our jewel. There is nothing
left;
Patience runs away, and impatience does
Seem appropriate for a mad dog: then is it a sin
To rush into the secret house of death,
Before death dares come to us? What do you think
women?
What, what! Good cheer! Why, what is it,
Charmian?
My noble girls! Ah, women, women, look,
Our lamp has used up its oil, it's out! Good sirs,
take heart,
We'll bury him; and then, what's brave, what's
noble,
Let's do with the way noble Romans do,
And make death proud to take us. Let's go:
The container of that huge spirit, his body, is cold
now:
Ah, women, women! Come; we have no friend
But tying up loose ends, and dying quickly.

ACT V

SCENE I. Alexandria. OCTAVIUS CAESAR's camp.

Enter OCTAVIUS CAESAR, AGRIPPA, DOLABELLA, MECAENAS, GALLUS, PROCULEIUS, and others, his council of war

OCTAVIUS CAESAR
Go to him, Dolabella, bid him yield;
Being so frustrate, tell him he mocks
The pauses that he makes.

Go to him, Dolabella, tell him to give in;
Being so frustrating, tell him he mocks
The pauses that he makes.

DOLABELLA
Caesar, I shall.

Caesar, I will.

Exit
Enter DERCETAS, with the sword of MARK ANTONY

OCTAVIUS CAESAR
Wherefore is that? and what art thou that darest
Appear thus to us?

What is that? And who are you that dares
Appear to us like that?

DERCETAS
I am call'd Dercetas;
Mark Antony I served, who best was worthy
Best to be served: whilst he stood up and spoke,
He was my master; and I wore my life
To spend upon his haters. If thou please
To take me to thee, as I was to him
I'll be to Caesar; if thou pleasest not,
I yield thee up my life.

I am called Dercetas:
I served Mark Antony, who was the best
I could have served: while he stood up and spoke,
He was my master; and I considered my life
Worth giving up on his haters. If you would like
To have me for you, the way I was to him
I'll be for Caesar; if you do not wish it,
I give my life up to you.

OCTAVIUS CAESAR
What is't thou say'st?

What are you saying?

DERCETAS
I say, O Caesar, Antony is dead.

I say, oh Caesar, Mark Antony is dead.

OCTAVIUS CAESAR
The breaking of so great a thing should make
A greater crack: the round world
Should have shook lions into civil streets,

The death of such a great thing should make
A louder crack: the round world
Should have shaken lions into the streets,

And citizens to their dens: the death of Antony

Is not a single doom; in the name lay
A moiety of the world.

DERCETAS
He is dead, Caesar:
Not by a public minister of justice,
Nor by a hired knife; but that self hand,
Which writ his honour in the acts it did,
Hath, with the courage which the heart did lend it,
Splitted the heart. This is his sword;
I robb'd his wound of it; behold it stain'd
With his most noble blood.

OCTAVIUS CAESAR
Look you sad, friends?
The gods rebuke me, but it is tidings
To wash the eyes of kings.

AGRIPPA
And strange it is,
That nature must compel us to lament
Our most persisted deeds.

MECAENAS
His taints and honours
Waged equal with him.

AGRIPPA
A rarer spirit never
Did steer humanity: but you, gods, will give us
Some faults to make us men. Caesar is touch'd.

MECAENAS
When such a spacious mirror's set before him,

He needs must see himself.

OCTAVIUS CAESAR
O Antony!
I have follow'd thee to this; but we do lance
Diseases in our bodies: I must perforce
Have shown to thee such a declining day,
Or look on thine; we could not stall together
In the whole world: but yet let me lament,
With tears as sovereign as the blood of hearts,
That thou, my brother, my competitor
Friend and companion in the front of war,
The arm of mine own body, and the heart

And citizens to their dens: the death of Mark Antony
Is not the doom of one man; in the name lay
A portion of the world.

He is dead, Caesar:
Not by a public minister of justice,
Not by an assassin; but that same hand
Which wrote his honor in the things it did,
Has, with the courage which his heart lended it,
Split the heart. This is his sword;
I pulled it out of his wound; see how it is stained
With his most noble blood.

Do you look sad, friends?
The gods may criticize me, but it is news
To make kings teary.

And it is strange,
That nature brings us to be sad
About things we were trying to do.

His flaws and qualities
Fought equally with him.

A more unique spirit never
Steered humanity: but you, gods, give us
A few flaws to make us mortal. Caesar is touched.

When such a big and wide mirror is placed in front of him,
He of course will see himself.

Oh, Antony!
I have pushed you to this; but we force out
Diseases in our bodies: I must have otherwise
Shown to you such a day,
Or look at yours; we could not coexist together
In the whole world: but still let me mourn,
With tears as genuine as the blood of hearts,
That you, my brother, my competitor
Friend and companion in the thick of war
The arm of my own body, and the heart

Where mine his thoughts did kindle,--that our stars,

Unreconciliable, should divide
Our equalness to this. Hear me, good friends--
But I will tell you at some meeter season:

Enter an Egyptian

The business of this man looks out of him;
We'll hear him what he says. Whence are you?

Egyptian
A poor Egyptian yet. The queen my mistress,
Confined in all she has, her monument,
Of thy intents desires instruction,
That she preparedly may frame herself
To the way she's forced to.

OCTAVIUS CAESAR
Bid her have good heart:
She soon shall know of us, by some of ours,
How honourable and how kindly we
Determine for her; for Caesar cannot live
To be ungentle.

Egyptian
So the gods preserve thee!

Exit

OCTAVIUS CAESAR
Come hither, Proculeius. Go and say,
We purpose her no shame: give her what comforts
The quality of her passion shall require,
Lest, in her greatness, by some mortal stroke

She do defeat us; for her life in Rome
Would be eternal in our triumph: go,
And with your speediest bring us what she says,
And how you find of her.

PROCULEIUS
Caesar, I shall.

Exit

OCTAVIUS CAESAR
Gallus, go you along.

Exit GALLUS

Where I shared thoughts with him, -- that our destiny,
Impossible to reconcile, would divide
Our equality to this. Hear me, good friends --
But I will tell you at a more appropriate time:

This man looks like he has important business;
We'll listen to what he has to say. Where did you come from?

I am still a poor Egyptian. My lady the queen,
Locked up with all she has, her monument,
Wants to know what you plan for her,
That she can prepare herself
To whatever you will force her.

Tell her to have confidence:
She will soon know from us, by some of ours,
How honorably and how kindly we
Have plans for her; for Caesar cannot live
To not be gentle.

May the gods care for you!

Come here, Proculeius. Go and say,
We have no shame for her: give her what comforts
She wants,
To prevent the possibility that, in her greatness, by some luck
She defeats us; for her life in Rome
Would be forever in our victory: go,
And as quickly as you can bring us what she says,
And how she is.

Caesar, I will.

Gallus, go with him.

Where's Dolabella,
To second Proculeius?

All
Dolabella!

OCTAVIUS CAESAR
Let him alone, for I remember now
How he's employ'd: he shall in time be ready.
Go with me to my tent; where you shall see
How hardly I was drawn into this war;
How calm and gentle I proceeded still
In all my writings: go with me, and see
What I can show in this.

Exeunt

Where's Dolabella,
To serve for Proculeius?

Dolabella!

Leave him alone, for I remember now
What he is doing: he will eventually be ready.
Go with me to my tent, where you will see
How rudely I was pulled into this war;
How calm and gentle I continued despite it
In all my writings: go with me, and see
What I can show in this.

SCENE II. Alexandria. A room in the monument.

Enter CLEOPATRA, CHARMIAN, and IRAS

CLEOPATRA
My desolation does begin to make
A better life. 'Tis paltry to be Caesar;
Not being Fortune, he's but Fortune's knave,
A minister of her will: and it is great
To do that thing that ends all other deeds;
Which shackles accidents and bolts up change;
Which sleeps, and never palates more the dug,
The beggar's nurse and Caesar's.

My ruin begins to make
A better life. It is not much to be Caesar;
Not being Fortune, he is only Fortune's servant,
Doing her will: and it is great
To do that thing that ends all other actions,
Which chains accidents and strengthens change;
Which sleeps, and never wants more dug up,
The beggar's nurse and Caesar's.

Enter, to the gates of the monument, PROCULEIUS, GALLUS and Soldiers

PROCULEIUS
Caesar sends greeting to the Queen of Egypt;
And bids thee study on what fair demands
Thou mean'st to have him grant thee.

Caesar sends greetings to the Queen of Egypt;
And wishes you to think about what fair demands
You mean to have him give you.

CLEOPATRA
What's thy name?

What is your name?

PROCULEIUS
My name is Proculeius.

My name is Proculeius.

CLEOPATRA
Antony
Did tell me of you, bade me trust you; but
I do not greatly care to be deceived,
That have no use for trusting. If your master
Would have a queen his beggar, you must tell him,
That majesty, to keep decorum, must
No less beg than a kingdom: if he please

To give me conquer'd Egypt for my son,
He gives me so much of mine own, as I
Will kneel to him with thanks.

Mark Antony
Told me about you, told me to trust you; but
I am not very much worried about being deceived,
Since I have no use for trusting. If your master
Wants a queen to beg him, you must tell him,
That royalty, to be proper, must
Beg for nothing less than a kingdom: if he would
be willing
To give me conquered Egypt for my son,
He gives me enough of my own, that I
Will kneel to him with thanks.

PROCULEIUS
Be of good cheer;
You're fall'n into a princely hand, fear nothing:
Make your full reference freely to my lord,
Who is so full of grace, that it flows over
On all that need: let me report to him
Your sweet dependency; and you shall find

Be cheerful;
You have fallen into a princely hand, do not fear:
Talk freely to my lord,
Who is so full of kindness, that it flows over
On everyone in need: let me report to him
Your humility; and you will find

A conqueror that will pray in aid for kindness,
Where he for grace is kneel'd to.

CLEOPATRA
Pray you, tell him
I am his fortune's vassal, and I send him
The greatness he has got. I hourly learn
A doctrine of obedience; and would gladly
Look him i' the face.

PROCULEIUS
This I'll report, dear lady.
Have comfort, for I know your plight is pitied
Of him that caused it.

GALLUS
You see how easily she may be surprised:

Here PROCULEIUS and two of the Guard ascend the monument by a ladder placed against a window, and, having descended, come behind CLEOPATRA. Some of the Guard unbar and open the gates

To PROCULEIUS and the Guard

Guard her till Caesar come.

Exit

IRAS
Royal queen!

CHARMIAN
O Cleopatra! thou art taken, queen:

CLEOPATRA
Quick, quick, good hands.

PROCULEIUS
Hold, worthy lady, hold:

Seizes and disarms her

Do not yourself such wrong, who are in this
Relieved, but not betray'd.

CLEOPATRA
What, of death too,
That rids our dogs of languish?

PROCULEIUS
Cleopatra,

A conqueror that will treat others with kindness,
When he is kneeled to graciously.

Please, tell him
I am his destiny's underling, and I send him
The greatness he has. Each hour I learn
A lesson of obedience; and would gladly
Look him in the face.

This I will report, dear lady.
Be comforted, for I know your situation is pitied
By him who caused it.

You see how easily she may be surprised:

Guard her until Caesar comes.

Royal queen!

Oh, Cleopatra! You have been captured, queen:

Drawing a dagger

Stop, worthy lady, stop:

Do not wrong yourself like this, who are
Kept safe, not betrayed.

What, from death too,
That releases our dogs from suffering?

Cleopatra,

Do not abuse my master's bounty by
The undoing of yourself: let the world see
His nobleness well acted, which your death
Will never let come forth.

CLEOPATRA
Where art thou, death?
Come hither, come! come, come, and take a queen
Worthy many babes and beggars!

PROCULEIUS
O, temperance, lady!

CLEOPATRA
Sir, I will eat no meat, I'll not drink, sir;
If idle talk will once be necessary,
I'll not sleep neither: this mortal house I'll ruin,
Do Caesar what he can. Know, sir, that I
Will not wait pinion'd at your master's court;
Nor once be chastised with the sober eye
Of dull Octavia. Shall they hoist me up
And show me to the shouting varletry
Of censuring Rome? Rather a ditch in Egypt
Be gentle grave unto me! rather on Nilus' mud
Lay me stark naked, and let the water-flies
Blow me into abhorring! rather make
My country's high pyramides my gibbet,
And hang me up in chains!

PROCULEIUS
You do extend
These thoughts of horror further than you shall
Find cause in Caesar.

Enter DOLABELLA

DOLABELLA
Proculeius,
What thou hast done thy master Caesar knows,

And he hath sent for thee: for the queen,
I'll take her to my guard.

PROCULEIUS
So, Dolabella,
It shall content me best: be gentle to her.

To CLEOPATRA

To Caesar I will speak what you shall please,

Do not abuse my master's generosity by
Destroying yourself: let the world see
His nobility acted upon, which your death
Will not allow to happen.

Where are you, death?
Come here, come! Come, come, and take a queen
Worth many babies and beggars!

Oh, calm down, lady!

Sir, I will eat no food, I won't drink, sir;
If talking is ever necessary,
I won't sleep either: my body I'll ruin,
Caesar can do what he likes. Know, sir, that I
Will not wait chained at your master's court;
Or once be criticized by the calm eye
Of dull Octavia. Will they put me up
And show me to the shouting people
Of critical Rome? I would rather a ditch in Egypt
Be a gentle grave to me! I would rather be lain
On the Nile's mud, and let the water-flies
Bite me to death! I would rather make
My country's high pyramids my scaffold,
And hang me up in chains!

You have much more elaborate
Thoughts of horror than you shall
Find reason to from Caesar.

Proculeius.
Caesar knows what you have done for your master,
And he has asked for you: for the queen,
I'll take her to my guard.

So, Dolabella,
I would like you to be gentle to her.

I will say to Caesar what you want,

If you'll employ me to him.

If you'll send me to him.

CLEOPATRA
Say, I would die.

Say I want to die.

Exeunt PROCULEIUS and Soldiers

DOLABELLA
Most noble empress, you have heard of me?

My noble empress, you have heard of me?

CLEOPATRA
I cannot tell.

I don't know.

DOLABELLA
Assuredly you know me.

You must know me.

CLEOPATRA
No matter, sir, what I have heard or known.

It does not matter, sir, what I have heard or known.

You laugh when boys or women tell their dreams;
Is't not your trick?

You laugh when boys or women tell their dreams;
Isn't that your trick?

DOLABELLA
I understand not, madam.

I don't understand, madam.

CLEOPATRA
I dream'd there was an Emperor Antony:
O, such another sleep, that I might see
But such another man!

I dreamed there was an Emperor Antony:
Oh, may I sleep like that again, so I might see
Another man like that!

DOLABELLA
If it might please ye,--

If it pleases you, --

CLEOPATRA
His face was as the heavens; and therein stuck
A sun and moon, which kept their course,
and lighted
The little O, the earth.

His face was like the sky; and in there was stuck
A sun and moon, which stayed on their path,
and lighted
The little circle, the Earth.

DOLABELLA
Most sovereign creature,--

Honorable ruler,--

CLEOPATRA
His legs bestrid the ocean: his rear'd arm
Crested the world: his voice was propertied
As all the tuned spheres, and that to friends;
But when he meant to quail and shake the orb,

His legs crossed the ocean: his raised arm
Was over the world: his voice was as loud
As any planet, and that to friends;
But when he meant to frighten and shake the sphere,

He was as rattling thunder. For his bounty,
There was no winter in't; an autumn 'twas

He was like rattling thunder. As for his wealth,
There was no winter in it; it was an autumn

That grew the more by reaping: his delights
Were dolphin-like; they show'd his back above

The element they lived in: in his livery
Walk'd crowns and crownets; realms and islands were

As plates dropp'd from his pocket.

DOLABELLA
Cleopatra!

CLEOPATRA
Think you there was, or might be, such a man
As this I dream'd of?

DOLABELLA
Gentle madam, no.

CLEOPATRA
You lie, up to the hearing of the gods.
But, if there be, or ever were, one such,

It's past the size of dreaming: nature wants stuff

To vie strange forms with fancy; yet, to imagine

And Antony, were nature's piece 'gainst fancy,

Condemning shadows quite.

DOLABELLA
Hear me, good madam.
Your loss is as yourself, great; and you bear it
As answering to the weight: would I might never

O'ertake pursued success, but I do feel,
By the rebound of yours, a grief that smites
My very heart at root.

CLEOPATRA
I thank you, sir,
Know you what Caesar means to do with me?

DOLABELLA
I am loath to tell you what I would you knew.

CLEOPATRA
Nay, pray you, sir,--

DOLABELLA

That grew the more it was harvested: his delights
Were like the playing of a dolphin; they showed his back above
The water they lived in: in his clothes
Were crowns and jewels; kingdoms and islands were
Like plates dropped from his pocket.

Cleopara!

Do you think there was, or might be, a man
Like this that I dreamed of?

Gentle lady, no.

You lie, in the hearing of the gods.
But, if there ever would be, or ever were, on like that
It's bigger than can be dreamed: nature needs stuff
To compete strange forms with imagination; yet, to imagine
And Antony, was nature's argument against imagination,
Driving the shadows away.

Listen to me, good madam.
Your loss is like you, important; and you carry it
According to your own importance: I wish that I might never
Go beyond chased success, but I do feel,
By the tragedy of yours, a grief that hits
The very bottom of my heart.

Thank you, sir.
Do you know what Caesar means to do to me?

I don't want to tell you what I want you to know.

No, please, sir,--

Though he be honourable,--

CLEOPATRA
He'll lead me, then, in triumph?

DOLABELLA
Madam, he will; I know't.

Flourish, and shout within, 'Make way there: Octavius Caesar!'
Enter OCTAVIUS CAESAR, GALLUS, PROCULEIUS, MECAENAS, SELEUCUS, and others of his Train

OCTAVIUS CAESAR
Which is the Queen of Egypt?

DOLABELLA
It is the emperor, madam.

CLEOPATRA kneels

OCTAVIUS CAESAR
Arise, you shall not kneel:
I pray you, rise; rise, Egypt.

CLEOPATRA
Sir, the gods
Will have it thus; my master and my lord
I must obey.

OCTAVIUS CAESAR
Take to you no hard thoughts:
The record of what injuries you did us,
Though written in our flesh, we shall remember
As things but done by chance.

CLEOPATRA
Sole sir o' the world,
I cannot project mine own cause so well
To make it clear; but do confess I have
Been laden with like frailties which before
Have often shamed our sex.

OCTAVIUS CAESAR
Cleopatra, know,
We will extenuate rather than enforce:
If you apply yourself to our intents,
Which towards you are most gentle, you shall find
A benefit in this change; but if you seek
To lay on me a cruelty, by taking
Antony's course, you shall bereave yourself

Even though he is honorable, --

He will parade me, then, in victory?

Lady, he will; I know it.

Which is the Queen of Egypt?

It is the emperor, madam.

Get up, you shall not kneel:
Please, get up; get up, Egypt.

Sir, the gods
Will have it like this; my master and my lord
I must obey.

Do not worry about
The record of the harm you did to us,
Even if permanent wounds, we shall remember
Them as pure happenstance.

Ruler of the world,
I cannot argue my own cause well enough
To make it clear; but do confess I have
Had to deal with similar weaknesses which before
Have often caused shame to women.

Cleopatra, know,
We will convince rather than force:
If you apply yourself to what we want,
Which are very gentle towards you, you will find
A benefit in this change; but if you try
To be cruel to me, by taking
Antony's path, you will rob yourself

Of my good purposes, and put your children

To that destruction which I'll guard them from,
If thereon you rely. I'll take my leave.

CLEOPATRA
And may, through all the world: 'tis yours; and we,

Your scutcheons and your signs of conquest, shall
Hang in what place you please. Here, my good lord.

OCTAVIUS CAESAR
You shall advise me in all for Cleopatra.

CLEOPATRA
This is the brief of money, plate, and jewels,
I am possess'd of: 'tis exactly valued;
Not petty things admitted. Where's Seleucus?

SELEUCUS
Here, madam.

CLEOPATRA
This is my treasurer: let him speak, my lord,
Upon his peril, that I have reserved
To myself nothing. Speak the truth, Seleucus.

SELEUCUS
Madam,
I had rather seal my lips, than, to my peril,
Speak that which is not.

CLEOPATRA
What have I kept back?

SELEUCUS
Enough to purchase what you have made known.

OCTAVIUS CAESAR
Nay, blush not, Cleopatra; I approve
Your wisdom in the deed.

CLEOPATRA
See, Caesar! O, behold,
How pomp is follow'd! mine will now be yours;
The ingratitude of this Seleucus does
Even make me wild: O slave, of no more trust

Than love that's hired! What, goest thou back?
thou shalt

From the opportunities I will give you, and put your children
To the destruction which I will protect them from,
If you trust me to. I'll leave now.

And may, through all the world, it is yours; and we,
Your trophies and your signs of conquest, shall
Be put in whatever place you please. Here, my good lord.

You will advice me what I should do for Cleopatra.

This is a list of money, precious metal, and jewels,
I have: it is exact and correct;
Nothing too minor. Where's Seleucus?

Here, madam.

This is my treasurer: let him speak, sir,
At his own risk, that I have kept
Nothing to myself. Tell the truth, Seleucus.

Madam,
I would rather stay silent, then, at my own risk,
Tell a lie.

What have I kept back?

Enough to buy what you have admitted to.

No, do not blush, Cleopatra; I approve
Your wisdom in doing so.

See, Caesar! Oh, look,
How wealth is followed! Mine will now be yours;
The ingratitude of Seleucus is enough to
Make me wild with anger: Oh slave, no more trustworthy
Than love that's paid for! What, are you going back, you will

Go back, I warrant thee; but I'll catch thine eyes,
Though they had wings: slave, soulless villain, dog!

O rarely base!

OCTAVIUS CAESAR
Good queen, let us entreat you.

CLEOPATRA
O Caesar, what a wounding shame is this,
That thou, vouchsafing here to visit me,
Doing the honour of thy lordliness
To one so meek, that mine own servant should
Parcel the sum of my disgraces by
Addition of his envy! Say, good Caesar,
That I some lady trifles have reserved,
Immoment toys, things of such dignity
As we greet modern friends withal; and say,
Some nobler token I have kept apart
For Livia and Octavia, to induce
Their mediation; must I be unfolded
With one that I have bred? The gods! it smites me
Beneath the fall I have.

To SELEUCUS

Prithee, go hence;
Or I shall show the cinders of my spirits
Through the ashes of my chance: wert thou a man,

Thou wouldst have mercy on me.

OCTAVIUS CAESAR
Forbear, Seleucus.

Exit SELEUCUS

CLEOPATRA
Be it known, that we, the greatest, are misthought

For things that others do; and, when we fall,
We answer others' merits in our name,
Are therefore to be pitied.

OCTAVIUS CAESAR
Cleopatra,
Not what you have reserved, nor what acknowledged,

Put we i' the roll of conquest: still be't yours,
Bestow it at your pleasure; and believe,

---

*Go back, I grant you; but I'll catch your eyes,
Even if they had wings: slave, soulless villain,
dog!
Oh unusually bad!*

Good queen, calm down.

*Oh Caesar, what a painful shame this is,
That you, coming here to visit me,
Doing the honor of your greatness
To one so humble, that my own servant would
Add on to my disgrace by
Adding on his envy! Say, good Caesar,
That I have reserved some minor lady things,
Little toys, with such dignity
That we use to greet modern friends; and say,
Some better items I have kept apart
For Livia and Octavia, to encourage
Their friendship; must I be revealed
By one of my servants? The gods! It hits me
Lower than I have already sunk.*

*Please, go away;
Or I will show the remaining coals of my spirits
Through the ashes of my destiny: if you were a
real man,
You would have mercy on me.*

Hold back, Seleucus.

*Let it be known that we, the greatest, are thought
wrongly
For things that others do; and, when we fall,
We are held responsible for things others did,
And should therefore be pitied.*

*Cleopatra,
None of what you have reserved, or what you have
admitted to,
Will we make a part of our booty: it is still yours,
Do what you like with it; and believe*

Caesar's no merchant, to make prize with you
Of things that merchants sold. Therefore be cheer'd;

Make not your thoughts your prisons: no, dear queen;

For we intend so to dispose you as
Yourself shall give us counsel. Feed, and sleep:
Our care and pity is so much upon you,
That we remain your friend; and so, adieu.

CLEOPATRA
My master, and my lord!

OCTAVIUS CAESAR
Not so. Adieu.

Flourish. Exeunt OCTAVIUS CAESAR and his train

CLEOPATRA
He words me, girls, he words me, that I should not

Be noble to myself: but, hark thee, Charmian.

Whispers to CHARMIAN

IRAS
Finish, good lady; the bright day is done,
And we are for the dark.

CLEOPATRA
Hie thee again:
I have spoke already, and it is provided;

Go put it to the haste.

CHARMIAN
Madam, I will.

Re-enter DOLABELLA

DOLABELLA
Where is the queen?

CHARMIAN
Behold, sir.

Exit

CLEOPATRA
Dolabella!

Caesar is no merchant, to make a prize of you
With things that merchants sell. Therefore, cheer up;
Do not turn your thoughts into your prisons: now, dear queen;
For we intend to treat you the way
You yourself want to be treated. Eat, and sleep:
Our care and·pity is so much upon you,
That we are still your friend; and so, goodbye.

My master, and my lord!

Oh, no, not like that. Farewell.

He persuades me, girls, her persuades me, that I should not
Do what I want: but, listen, Charmian.

Finish, good lady; the bright day is done,
And we are now in the dark.

Go now again:
I have spoken it already, and it has been taken care of;
Go make it happen quickly.

Madam, I will.

Where's the queen?

See, sir.

Dolabella!

DOLABELLA
Madam, as thereto sworn by your command,
Which my love makes religion to obey,
I tell you this: Caesar through Syria
Intends his journey; and within three days
You with your children will he send before:
Make your best use of this: I have perform'd
Your pleasure and my promise.

Madam, as you made me promise to tell,
Which my love commands me to obey,
I tell you this: Caesar intends to travel
Through Syria; and within three days
You and your children will be sent in front of him:
Do your best with this information: I have done
What you wanted and what I promised.

CLEOPATRA
Dolabella,
I shall remain your debtor.

Dolabella,
I will be in your debt.

DOLABELLA
I your servant,
Adieu, good queen; I must attend on Caesar.

I will stay your servant,
Farewell, good queen; I must serve Caesar.

CLEOPATRA
Farewell, and thanks.

Farewell, and thanks.

Exit DOLABELLA

Now, Iras, what think'st thou?
Thou, an Egyptian puppet, shalt be shown
In Rome, as well as I mechanic slaves
With greasy aprons, rules, and hammers, shall
Uplift us to the view; in their thick breaths,
Rank of gross diet, shall be enclouded,
And forced to drink their vapour.

Now, Iras, what do you think?
You, an Egyptian puppet, will be shown
In Rome, as well as me, mechanic slaves
With greasy aprons, rulers, and hammers, will
Lift us up to be seen; in their thick breaths
Smelly with their diet, will be clouded,
And forced to drink their mist.

IRAS
The gods forbid!

May the gods forbid!

CLEOPATRA
Nay, 'tis most certain, Iras: saucy lictors
Will catch at us, like strumpets; and scald rhymers
Ballad us out o' tune: the quick comedians
Extemporally will stage us, and present
Our Alexandrian revels; Antony
Shall be brought drunken forth, and I shall see
Some squeaking Cleopatra boy my greatness
I' the posture of a whore.

No, it is certain, Iras: sauce women
Will torment us, like sluts; and musicians
Sing us out of tune: the quick comedians
Will make plays based on us, and present
Our parties in Alexandria; Antony
Will be brought out drunk, and I will see
Some squeaking boy as Cleopatra, my greatness
In the position of a whore.

IRAS
O the good gods!

Oh, good gods!

CLEOPATRA
Nay, that's certain.

No, it's certain.

IRAS

I'll never see 't; for, I am sure, my nails
Are stronger than mine eyes.

CLEOPATRA
Why, that's the way
To fool their preparation, and to conquer
Their most absurd intents.

Re-enter CHARMIAN

Now, Charmian!
Show me, my women, like a queen: go fetch
My best attires: I am again for Cydnus,
To meet Mark Antony: sirrah Iras, go.
Now, noble Charmian, we'll dispatch indeed;

And, when thou hast done this chare, I'll give thee
leave
To play till doomsday. Bring our crown and all.

Wherefore's this noise?

Exit IRAS. A noise within
Enter a Guardsman

Guard
Here is a rural fellow
That will not be denied your highness presence:
He brings you figs.

CLEOPATRA
Let him come in.

Exit Guardsman

What poor an instrument
May do a noble deed! he brings me liberty.
My resolution's placed, and I have nothing
Of woman in me: now from head to foot
I am marble-constant; now the fleeting moon
No planet is of mine.

Re-enter Guardsman, with Clown bringing in a basket

Guard
This is the man.

CLEOPATRA
Avoid, and leave him.

I will never see it; for, I am sure, my nails
Are stronger than my eyes.

Why, that's the way
To spoil their plans, and to overcome
What they want to do.

Now, Charmian!
Show me, my women, like a queen: go fetch
My best clothes: I am going to Cydnus
To meet Mark Antony: sweet Iras, go.
Now, noble Charmian, we'll find a solution
indeed:
And, when you have done this chore, I'll give you
permission
To play until the end of the world. Bring our
crown and all.
What is the meaning of this noise?

Here is a farmer
Who demands to see your highness:
He brings you figs.

Let him in.

What poor tool
May do a great thing! He brings me freedom.
I am decided, and I no longer have anything
Womanly in me: now from head to foot
I am as solid as marble; I am not like the moon
Changing.

This is the man.

Go, and leave him.

Exit Guardsman

Hast thou the pretty worm of Nilus there,
That kills and pains not?

*Do you have the pretty snake of the Nile there,
That kills without causing pain?*

Clown

Truly, I have him: but I would not be the party
that should desire you to touch him, for his biting
is immortal; those that do die of it do seldom or
never recover.

*Yes, I have him: but I would not be the one
that wanted you to touch him, for his biting
will kill; those that die of it rarely or
never recover.*

CLEOPATRA

Rememberest thou any that have died on't?

Do you remember anyone who has died of it?

Clown

Very many, men and women too. I heard of one of
them no longer than yesterday: a very honest woman,
but something given to lie; as a woman should not
do, but in the way of honesty: how she died of the
biting of it, what pain she felt: truly, she makes
a very good report o' the worm; but he that will
believe all that they say, shall never be saved by
half that they do: but this is most fallible, the
worm's an odd worm.

*Many, men and women too. I heard about one of
them only yesterday: a very honest woman,
but sometimes a liar; the way a woman should not
be, but in the way of honesty: how she died from
it's biting, what pain she felt: truly, she makes
a very good report of the snake; but he that will
believe all they say, will never be saved by
half that they do: but this is most unreliable, the
snake's a strange snake.*

CLEOPATRA

Get thee hence; farewell.

Go away from here, goodbye.

Clown

I wish you all joy of the worm.

Good luck with the snake.

Setting down his basket

CLEOPATRA

Farewell.

Farewell.

Clown

You must think this, look you, that the worm will
do his kind.

*You must think this, now, that the snake will
act as snakes do.*

CLEOPATRA

Ay, ay; farewell.

Yes, yes; farewell.

Clown

Look you, the worm is not to be trusted but in the

keeping of wise people; for, indeed, there is no
goodness in worm.

*Look, now, the snake should not be trusted but in
the
keeping of wise people; for, indeed, there is now
goodness in snakes.*

CLEOPATRA

Take thou no care; it shall be heeded.

Clown
Very good. Give it nothing, I pray you, for it is
not worth the feeding.

CLEOPATRA
Will it eat me?

Clown
You must not think I am so simple but I know the

devil himself will not eat a woman: I know that a
woman is a dish for the gods, if the devil dress her
not. But, truly, these same whoreson devils do the

gods great harm in their women; for in every ten

that they make, the devils mar five.

CLEOPATRA
Well, get thee gone; farewell.

Clown
Yes, forsooth: I wish you joy o' the worm.

Exit
Re-enter IRAS with a robe, crown, & c

CLEOPATRA
Give me my robe, put on my crown; I have
Immortal longings in me: now no more

The juice of Egypt's grape shall moist this lip:
Yare, yare, good Iras; quick. Methinks I hear
Antony call; I see him rouse himself
To praise my noble act; I hear him mock
The luck of Caesar, which the gods give men
To excuse their after wrath: husband, I come:

Now to that name my courage prove my title!
I am fire and air; my other elements
I give to baser life. So; have you done?
Come then, and take the last warmth of my lips.
Farewell, kind Charmian; Iras, long farewell.

Kisses them. IRAS falls and dies

Have I the aspic in my lips? Dost fall?
If thou and nature can so gently part,

Don't worry, your advice will be listened to.

*Very good. Give it nothing to eat, please, for it is
not worth feeding.*

Will it eat me?

*You must not think I am so silly as to not know
that
devil himself will not eat a woman: I know that a
woman is a dish for the gods, if the devil does not
cook her. But, truly, these same [insult] devils do
the
gods much harm with their women; for in every
ten
that they make, the devils spoil five.*

Go away now, goodbye.

Yes

*Give me my robe, put on my crown; I have
Longings that will never die in me: now never
again
The juice of Egypt's grape will dampen this lip:
Lightly, lightly, good Iras; quick. I think I hear
Antony call; I see him get up
To praise my noble act; I hear him mock
Caesar's luck, which the gods give men
To excuse their anger afterwards: husband, I
come:
Now may my courage make that title real!
I am fire and air; my other elements
I give away to lower life. So; are you done?
Come then, and take the last warmth of my lips.
Goodbye, kind Charmian; Iras, goodbye.*

*Do I have the poison in my lips? Did you fall?
If you and nature can so gently separate,*

The stroke of death is as a lover's pinch,
Which hurts, and is desired. Dost thou lie still?
If thus thou vanishest, thou tell'st the world
It is not worth leave-taking.

CHARMIAN
Dissolve, thick cloud, and rain; that I may say,
The gods themselves do weep!

CLEOPATRA
This proves me base:
If she first meet the curled Antony,
He'll make demand of her, and spend that kiss
Which is my heaven to have. Come, thou mortal
wretch,

To an asp, which she applies to her breast

With thy sharp teeth this knot intrinsicate
Of life at once untie: poor venomous fool
Be angry, and dispatch. O, couldst thou speak,
That I might hear thee call great Caesar ass
Unpolicied!

CHARMIAN
O eastern star!

CLEOPATRA
Peace, peace!
Dost thou not see my baby at my breast,
That sucks the nurse asleep?

CHARMIAN
O, break! O, break!

CLEOPATRA
As sweet as balm, as soft as air, as gentle,--
O Antony!--Nay, I will take thee too.

Applying another asp to her arm

What should I stay--

Dies

CHARMIAN
In this vile world? So, fare thee well.
Now boast thee, death, in thy possession lies
A lass unparalle'd. Downy windows, close;
And golden Phoebus never be beheld

*The stroke of death is like the pinch of a lover,
That is hurts, and is wanted. Do you lie still?
If this is how you die, you tell the world
It is not worth saying goodbye.*

*Dissolve, thick cloud, and rain; so that I can say,
The gods themselves do weep!*

*This would ruin me:
If she is the first to meet the dead Antony,
He'll demand from her, and spend that kiss
Which is my heaven to have. Come, you killing
beast,*

*Undo the knot of life with your sharp teeth
At once: poor venomous fool
Be angry, and kill. Oh, if only you could speak,
That I could hear you call the big ass Caesar
Defeated!*

Oh eastern star!

*Quiet, quiet!
Do you not see my baby at my breast,
That sucks the nurse to her sleep?*

Oh, break! Oh, break!

*As sweet as ointment, as soft as air, as gentle,--
O Antony! -- No, I will take you too.*

What should I stay--

*In this ugly world? So, goodbye.
Now you may brag, death, for you have
A woman like no other. Eyelids, close;
And may never be seen again*

Of eyes again so royal! Your crown's awry;
I'll mend it, and then play.

*Eyes so royal! Your crown is crooked;
I'll fix it, and then play.*

Enter the Guard, rushing in

First Guard
Where is the queen?

Where is the queen?

CHARMIAN
Speak softly, wake her not.

Speak softly, don't wake her.

First Guard
Caesar hath sent--

Caesar has sent--

CHARMIAN
Too slow a messenger.

A messenger that is too slow.

Applies an asp

O, come apace, dispatch! I partly feel thee.

Oh, come quickly, death! I can feel part of you.

First Guard
Approach, ho! All's not well: Caesar's beguiled.

Come, hey! Things are not good: Caesar's been tricked.

Second Guard
There's Dolabella sent from Caesar; call him.

Here is Dolabella sent by Caesar; call him.

First Guard
What work is here! Charmian, is this well done?

What work is here? Charmian, has this been done?

CHARMIAN
It is well done, and fitting for a princess
Descended of so many royal kings.
Ah, soldier!

*It is well done, and suitable for a princess
Descended from so many royal kings.
Ah, soldier!*

Dies

Re-enter DOLABELLA

DOLABELLA
How goes it here?

How are things here?

Second Guard
All dead.

All dead.

DOLABELLA
Caesar, thy thoughts
Touch their effects in this: thyself art coming
To see perform'd the dreaded act which thou
So sought'st to hinder.

*Caesar, your thoughts
Touch your effects in this: you yourself have come
To see happen that terrible act which you
Tried so hard to prevent.*

Within 'A way there, a way for Caesar!'
Re-enter OCTAVIUS CAESAR and all his train marching

DOLABELLA
O sir, you are too sure an augurer;
That you did fear is done.

Oh, sir, you are too good a fortuneteller
What you feared would happen is done.

OCTAVIUS CAESAR
Bravest at the last,
She levell'd at our purposes, and, being royal,
Took her own way. The manner of their deaths?
I do not see them bleed.

Bravest at the end,
She fought against our purposes, and, being royal,
Took her own way. How did they die?
I do not see them bleed.

DOLABELLA
Who was last with them?

Who was the last person with them?

First Guard
A simple countryman, that brought her figs:
This was his basket.

A simple peasant, that brought her figs:
This was his basket.

OCTAVIUS CAESAR
Poison'd, then.

Poisoned, then.

First Guard
O Caesar,
This Charmian lived but now; she stood and spake:

I found her trimming up the diadem
On her dead mistress; tremblingly she stood
And on the sudden dropp'd.

Oh Caesar,
Charmian lived until a moment ago; she stood and
spoke:
I found her fixing the crown
On her dead lady; she stood shaking
And suddenly dropped.

OCTAVIUS CAESAR
O noble weakness!
If they had swallow'd poison, 'twould appear
By external swelling: but she looks like sleep,

As she would catch another Antony
In her strong toil of grace.

Oh noble weakness!
If they had swallowed poison, it would appear
By swelling on the outside: but she looks like she's
asleep,
As if she could catch another Antony
By her strong grace.

DOLABELLA
Here, on her breast,
There is a vent of blood and something blown:
The like is on her arm.

Here, on her breast,
There is a trial of blood and something punctured:
There is something similar on her arm.

First Guard
This is an aspic's trail: and these fig-leaves
Have slime upon them, such as the aspic leaves
Upon the caves of Nile.

This is an asp's trail: and these fig leaves
Have slime on them, the way the asp leaves trails
On the caves of the Nile.

OCTAVIUS CAESAR

Most probable
That so she died; for her physician tells me
She hath pursued conclusions infinite
Of easy ways to die. Take up her bed;
And bear her women from the monument:
She shall be buried by her Antony:
No grave upon the earth shall clip in it
A pair so famous. High events as these
Strike those that make them; and their story is
No less in pity than his glory which
Brought them to be lamented. Our army shall
In solemn show attend this funeral;
And then to Rome. Come, Dolabella, see
High order in this great solemnity.

Exeunt

It is likely
That she died that way; for her doctor tells me
She has researched many ways
That one can painlessly die. Take up her bed;
And carry her women from the monument:
She shall be buried by her Mark Antony:
No grave on the earth shall have in it
A pair as famous. High events like these
Cut down those who make them, and their story is
No less pitiful than his glory that
Brought them to be mourned. Our army shall
Solemnly attend this funeral;
And then on to Rome. Come, Dolabella, see
The noble order in this great seriousness.